Erie Tales #15: Classic Monsters

Presented by
The Great Lakes Association of Horror Writers

Edited by
Michael Cieslak

www.glahw.com

This anthology is a work of fiction. Names, characters, places, and scenarios are the products of the authors' imagination. Any resemblance to actual persons living or dead, places, or events is purely coincidental.

Collection and editorial content
Copyright © 2023 Great Lakes Association of Horror Writers

Cover art copyright © 2022 Don England

Great Lakes Association of Horror Writers logo by Dave Harvey Copyright © 2007 Great Lakes Association of Horror Writers

All rights reserved. No portion of this publication can be reproduced by any means without the prior written permission from the authors of the work and from the Great Lakes Association of Horror Writers except for the use of brief quotations in a book review.

First Printing, 2023
Great Lakes Association of Horror Writers
www.glahw.com

THE DREADFUL SISTERS WHO REMAIN copyright © 2022 Peggy Christie
THESE THINGS MOVE IN CYCLES copyright © 2022 M.C. St. John
AN EYE FOR BEAUTY copyright © 2022 R D Doan
THAT WON'T HOLD UP IN COURT copyright © 2022 Jen Haeger
NO COUNTRY FOR OLD BLOBS copyright © 2022 Matthew Tansek
ANOTHER LINE copyright © 2022 Melodie Bolt
SUBSTITUTE copyright © 2022 J.M. Van Horn

ISBN: 9798375583969

Table of Contents

Table of Contents	iii
Introduction	i
The Dreadful Sisters Who Remain *by Peggy Christie*	1
These Things Move In Cycles *by M.C. St. John*	15
An Eye for Beauty *by R D Doan*	27
That Won't Hold Up in Court *by Jen Haeger*	37
No Country for Old Blobs *by Matthew Tansek*	47
Another Line *by Melodie Bolt*	63
Substitute *by J.M. Van Horn*	69
Contributing Authors	77
About GLAHW	81

This page is intentionally blank

ACKNOWLEDGMENTS

All of the members of the GLAHW, especially those who submitted work to this year's anthology.

The family members/Con widows and widowers who allow us the time and privacy to write, attend functions, and all of the other writing and horror related activities which occupy us.

The extended GLAHW family, including the traveling band of authors, artists, and fans we see on the convention circuit.

MontiLee Stormer for her tireless efforts formatting and finalizing the publishing details of not just the Erie Tales anthologies but all of the GLAHW publications.

Don England for his amazing artwork -- this is someone who turns in a publication worthy "rough draft" and then proceeds to improve on what was already amazing.

This page is intentionally blank

Introduction

Generally speaking, I am not a fan of reboots and re-imaginings.

This is doubly true when it applies to the horror genre.

The problem is that most of them take a story which has limited (or often no) relation to the original and try to pass it off as the successor to the much superior original. Often, the only reason that they are using the title in the first place is to cash in on name recognition.*

However (and this is a big one), that really only applies to films and television.

Literature has a much better track record when it comes to exploring an idea from a previous work and then expanding upon it or taking it in a new direction. Different authors have delved into everything from Shakespeare to Greek Literature, Classics to Fairy Tales and placed their own spin on them.

In other words, the book was better.

Cue this year's theme announcement: Classic Monsters. The fine authors of the Great Lakes Association of Horror Writers focused their gazes on monsters that every reader, not just the horror fanatics, will be familiar with. Interestingly, the authors avoided the big three Universal Monsters, but then Dracula, The Wolfman, and Frankenstein's Monster have more than their fair share of additional tales. You'll be pleasantly surprised by those that do show up in these pages.

Congratulations to Peggy Christie whose story "The Dreadful Sisters Who Remain" was selected by the members as their favorite and which earned the author a professional rate payment of $0.06 per word.

Thank you for joining us once again. Settle in and prepare to look at some old friends in a new light.

And, as always, don't be afraid. Be terrified.

Michael Cieslak
Editor, Erie Tales #15

*I fully acknowledge that there are some brilliant remakes out there, some of which even surpass the originals. I'm looking at you The Thing, The Fly, The Blob ... so maybe just things made in the 80s with the article "The" in the title. Oh, no wait, Invasion of the Body Snatchers.

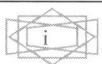

Special Congratulations to...

The Great Lakes Association of Horror Writers offers pro-rate payment to the author of one of our submissions. Once the stories had been compiled, they were distributed to the members. The votes have been tabulated, the ties broken, and the winner chosen. Congratulations to **Peggy Christie**, author of "The Dreadful Sisters Who Remain".

Now's the time to run.

The Dreadful Sisters Who Remain

by Peggy Christie

"I can't say I'm sorry because it would be a lie. And despite the horrors I have visited upon you and the world, I am not, and never will be, a liar."

She offered him a sympathetic smile, her pointed fangs glistening in the wan light. "Everything you have spoken since we met has been a lie, doctor, including your name. I will only recognize your lack of remorse because that is the only truth you carry. And you will die with that truth on your lips."

She accepted the surrender in his stare. Euryale gripped his throat, digging her thick fingers into his soft flesh. With one quick twist, she removed his head from his neck. His body crumpled to the floor and when she dropped the head, it landed on the corpse with a soft squish. Euryale wiped the man's blood on the remnants of rags he'd allowed her for modesty's sake. His comfort, not hers.

Her sister, Stheno, moved next to her, glaring down at the dead human. She clicked her claws together, their sharp ticks echoing through the cold laboratory. She relaxed her wings and folded them against her back.

"Looks like you own me one, Lee."

Euryale sighed her exasperation. "Sister, please refrain from speaking my name in such a crude manner, at least when we are alone."

"You got it, Yer-eye-uh-lee. But I don't think we're alone."

The soft shuffle of stockinged feet approached the pair. The source belonged to the doctor's unfortunate deceased wife. She moved without purpose, her vacant gaze focusing on nothing and no one as she walked. She spent most of her days in this repetitive stupor, trailing back and forth through the empty rooms of the house.

As she passed the sisters, she turned her gaze fell to husband's lifeless body. For the first time since she woke as a prisoner here, Euryale saw a flicker of emotion scuttle across the woman's face without the assistance of a fresh victim's blood. Her features scrunched together, distorting her expression from nonchalance to agony within seconds.

The woman's mouth gaped and a whisper, like the dying cry of an injured animal, echoed through the room as she threw herself on top of her husband. She clutched his shirt, shook him as if he were sleeping, desperate to wake him.

"It appears a sliver of soul clung to her during her resurrection."

"It's rare but does happen from time to time."

"You have seen such a thing?"

Stheno nodded. "Centuries ago when that madman kidnapped me. His daughter's soul clung to her physical form causing an unbreakable psychosis. He had to destroy her in the end."

"What a waste."

The wife finally noticed the two sisters standing over her. She reached for Stheno, clinging to her thick legs. A ragged whimper escaped her throat begging for help. With no response she turned to Euryale, and recognition widened her eyes.

She grabbed the tattered clothing at Euryale's waist, ripping them further. The wound in her right side glistened, still not completely healed. The wife's arm shot up, scrabbling for the incision, eager to tear it open again.

Scales popping up like gooseflesh, Euryale slapped the woman, who moaned as she fell back. Undeterred, she rose to her knees and lunged forward, the desperation in her eyes bordering on insanity. Euryale grabbed the woman by her long scraggly hair then lifted her off the ground. She thrashed in Euryale's grip.

Raising the woman above her head and whipping her down, like shaking water from a drenched garment, Euryale separated the woman's head from her body. The pop of her spine as it shattered drowned out the rending of flesh and skin and tendons. The wife's body collapsed on top of her husband's and Euryale tossed the detached head atop them both.

Stheno laid a hand on Lee's shoulder.

"Let's get the hell out of here."

"Stheno, please, must you--"

"Fine, fine." She cleared her throat. "And now, sister, let us take our leave of this decrepit dwelling and find respite so you may fully heal and regain your strength."

Euryale smirked. "Thank--"

"AKA, let's blow this popsicle stand!"

Euryale shook her head. "Come, Stef. Let us go home."

"So Ionian planned this all along? Using your blood to bring back his wife?"

Euryale exhaled. "Yes, but his name wasn't Ionian. Just another link in the chain of lies he made to bind me in trust."

Stef chuckled. Euryale glared at her older sister. "What is so amusing?"

"Exactly how old are you, Lee? A centuries old immortal falling for a human's tricks."

"Surely you remember you are older than I. How is it that you could not see through his ruse either?"

Stef opened her mouth to reply then quickly snapped it shut. The sisters left the lab and the house behind, walking hand in hand as the setting sun painted the sky orange, red, and purple.

"There are only two left, my dear. Once they've met with justice, we can leave this place and go on with our lives."

Emily could only mewl, a deep saddened keening that Euryale had come to recognize as resignation. Why the doctor couldn't, or wouldn't, acknowledge it could only be explained by the joy he felt at her return.

Or he was insane. By Euryale's standards, anyone who raised the dead back to life was bound to a mindset of fury.

From her shackled nook, Euryale watched the doctor fawn over his dead bride, caressing the flaky skin of her blue cheek, kissing her cracked hands. He pulled a handkerchief from his pocket and wiped the fresh blood from her lips. Emily turned away, as if embarrassed for having bitten the throat from the man lying at their feet. The doctor gently pulled her chin so she would meet his gaze.

"You never have to be sorry for this, my darling. He died that night when he dared to touch you. They all did. It's just that death showed up a little late, that's all."

Emily patted his hand but again looked down at the body, the fresh blood glistening in the fluorescent lights. Though her speech never recovered, after a kill she moved like a regular human, even expressing love for her husband. And yet, within hours, she would return to the shambling, vacant-minded corpse that he'd resurrected a month prior.

The doctor approached Euryale, a shameful half-smile dominating his expression.

"I know I ask a lot of you, Euryale, and I promise it's almost over.

But for now, I must take more."

She leaned back against the wall and turned her gaze away from him. "Why do you bother to speak, Doctor? You do as you will, in spite of my protests and threats."

"You understand why, don't you? You see the proof standing before your very eyes. Emily, my dearest Emily, has returned."

"That is not your wife."

"Well, of course she is."

Euryale turned her head to look at him. During her first week of captivity, her mind raged, planning and plotting the doctor's demise the moment she could free herself of these charmed shackles. But as she stared at his gaunt face, studied his shaking hands, and noted the welling of unshed tears in his eyes, she sighed.

"Perhaps this delusion fuels your quest for vengeance, but I have grown weary. Take your dose of blood and leave me be."

She turned away from him again and listened as he fumbled with his implements. She'd stopped showing her fangs and scales to him weeks ago but whenever he cut into her flesh, they showed themselves against her will. The doctor flinched every time, amazed and horrified by her true form. But was never sorry.

"I'm hoping to lure the last two simultaneously so I will need to procure more this time."

The cold steel of the scalpel bit into her flesh. She couldn't help but watch as he gathered her blood into a conical flask instead of a test tube. He filled it to the base of its neck before pressing his handkerchief against the wound. Though unnecessary, Euryale supposed his humanity, such as it was, instinctually tried to help as much as it hurt.

"Ah, yes. This should work. I've been studying the ancient parchments. I'm hoping this amount will give my Emily a more…permanent temperament."

"You cannot be serious."

"I would never lie about such a thing."

Euryale could feel a cruel sneer stretch across her face.

"Doctor, I am confused by two things. One, do you honestly believe your Emily will ever return as she was?"

"Of course, I do. Otherwise, why would I even try?"

Euryale scoffed, an incredulous snicker echoing through the lab. The doctor remained unshaken. Still, he did stop working on his mixture to turn and look at her.

"And what is the second thing that confuses you?"

Euryale stared at him. She could feel the heat rising to her face; scales popped up across her skin like gooseflesh and her fangs emerged.

"Do you honestly believe, doctor, that when this is over, when your revenge is complete, that I will allow either of you to live?"

His already milky skin paled to the color of ash left in an ancient hearth. He adjusted the tie at his neck and cleared his throat. The shaky smile couldn't hide his fear. He turned back to his experiment.

"As long as those shackles hold and the spells remain intact, I'm afraid you can't do anything to harm either of us."

She looked from the metal bindings at her wrists to the scrawled pictograms within the niche.

"I suppose that is true, doctor. But you must have forgotten. Though I am a rare and ancient beast, I am not the only one."

His hand stopped, hovering over the flask as a white powder fell from his fingertips. His shaking worsened and his bravado slipped.

"We are in a most secret place, I'm afraid. By the time anyone finds it, Emily and I will be gone. So I must implore you to refrain from these vague threats, and let me concentrate."

She sighed again, too tired to engage in such trivialities with this human. He was right in at least one aspect. He had her trapped and powerless against his whims. Unless an outside force worked in her favor, Euryale could do nothing to change her circumstances.

Within minutes, the doctor finished his concoction and stored it in a small refrigerator under one of the lab tables. That same sheepish grin returned as he picked up a clean scalpel and test tube before approaching her left side. She glared at him.

"I thought you wanted to mete out justice in a different fashion, doctor."

His gaze flicked to the left where Emily stood, staring down at the dead man at her feet. The doctor frowned; the only time she'd ever seen him look disgusted. He pressed his fingers against her ribs and plunged the scalpel between two of them. She clenched her jaw to keep her fangs from extending. Immortality didn't make her impervious to pain.

He began to fill the tube with more of her blood, though this fluid held a ribbon of black ooze that swirled with a life of its own.

"Be careful, doctor. Even a drop of that will fell the largest and strongest of men, let alone a coward of the highest echelon."

He jerked the half-filled tube away before quickly placing it in a metal rack. Wiping his dry hand on his smock, he strode over to Emily who already started showing signs of a zombified state. Glancing over his shoulder at Euryale, the doctor escorted his wife out of the laboratory.

"Come, my dear. Let's get you more comfortable and out of this dreadful room. Perhaps some tea on the veranda?"

Emily moaned, allowing him to lead her back into the house. Euryale laughed, a humorless guttural cackle, as the heavy steel door shut her in darkness.

Euryale awoke to a searing pain in her right side. She could feel the warmth of her own blood as it oozed down her flank. The cool metal of various restraints pressed against her body, rendering her immobile. Blinking, she rolled her eyes to the left. The mundane implements of a scientific laboratory filled the fuzzy edges of her vision: two rolling gurneys, multiple low tables covered with medical instruments, and every shape and size of glass and metal beakers filled with various liquids.

The body of a woman on the table beside her, however, struck her as the farthest thing from ordinary she could ever have encountered.

Human, from what Euryale could determine. Long, thin, blonde hair; a smattering of pale freckles marked her cheeks and shoulders. What had likely once been a visage of beauty sunk into darkened eye sockets and rotten flesh. The advanced decay of the body made identification problematic but even if a living woman laid there, Euryale would have no way of knowing her.

She did recognize the man fussing over the corpse. Dr. Ionian crossed Euryale's path no more than seven days ago. He'd impressed her as highly intelligent, passionate, and driven. She hadn't encountered another like him in decades. That plus his name, and the city in which he lived, tugged at her sense of nostalgia and longing for her homeland of Greece.

"Your name is Dr. Ionian and you live in Ionia?"

He chuckled. "People mistakenly believe my family founded the town when, truth be told, it's the opposite. My ancestors renamed themselves after the town. Apparently, a scandal forced them to flee their previous home, and in order to hide from the pursuing law, they changed the family name."

"How fascinating. What had they done?"

"I'm not familiar with all the particulars. My grandfather was rather tight lipped about the whole ordeal. But it had to do with…"

He paused to look around, as if afraid someone might overhear. He placed his hands on either side of his mouth and whispered, "Medical experimentation."

She stared at him, her eyes wide, and he laughed.

"My wife always got a kick out of the old stories. She'd pretend to be shocked, threaten to tell the town council so they'd come with their pitchforks and torches."

"You should not make light of that. If I have learned nothing else in my life, it is that humans are easily frightened and will destroy anything that makes them feel weak."

"You speak as if you're not part of the human race, too."

She'd nearly forgotten herself during the conversation, but he smiled and continued.

"You are correct. It was just our way of coping with such nasty rumors, which still survive to this day. My Emily's jokes helped soothe the pain."

"You must love her a lot."

"I did. I do. Unfortunately, she's been gone for two years. I must admit I'm still struggling with the loss."

His face flushed a bright pink and he rubbed a roughened hand across his stubbly chin. "Please forgive me. I've prattled on too long about my problems. Tell me about you. What brings you to this small community out in the middle of Nowhere, Michigan?"

That was the beginning of their friendship. Or what Euryale believed to be friendship. She'd gone too long since bonding with anyone aside from her remaining sister. They'd both understood the power of loss, how death could darken the souls of those left behind. After that human murdered their younger sister, she and Stef had wandered the world, bitter and angry with the human race. They meted out justice against anyone who'd given even the slightest offense.

Eventually, they parted ways, each tired of the other's company and their shared hate. Euryale held that feeing close, letting it warm her through her journeys. But every few centuries, she'd meet a human that showed her another characteristic of its species, one that chose love over fear, hope over despair. Dr. Ionian allowed Euryale a glimpse into that world with each meeting.

This milquetoast man hardly screamed 'mad scientist' yet here he sat, claiming a horrific family history worthy of the myths of her youth. Unfortunately for her, lowering her guard, forgetting the duplicitous nature of the human animal, would prove to be her downfall.

"Are you familiar with the Greek poet, Hesiod, and his poems of the Gorgons?"

She blinked, yet again surprised. Not by the fact this man knew of the tales. Nearly every human she encountered knew the stories in one form or another. It was the way he asked the question, how his eyebrows raised as he looked at her; how he leaned forward to create the pretense of intimacy. Not until she felt the sharp pain in her thigh did she realize her mistake. Her gasp came out more of a hiss and Dr. Ionian pulled back, still holding the syringe in his left hand. His didn't display malice, only sympathy. He felt sorry for her, an emotion she hated more than any other.

"I am sorry, my dear. I need your help and considering who and what you are, I knew you would deny my request. I promise I won't hurt you. At least no more than might be necessary to complete my experiments."

"You...fool." Her words stuck between her teeth. The drug he'd administered must be powerful indeed to subdue even a Gorgon.

That was her last memory before the present moment, Dr. Ionian bent over a dead woman, and she shackled to this table. It finally dawned on her the corpse was Emily, the doctor's dead wife. Despite the modern marvel of embalming, the grave had not been kind to the woman. Either the doctor's delusion prevented him from noticing, or he simply didn't care. Either way, with Euryale's blood, the rotting corpse would soon be up and mobile.

Gerald sat in the police briefing room, shoulders slumped, his face still wet with tears and his wife's blood. The steaming cup of coffee sat untouched before him. The investigator across the table, a young inexperienced man of no more than twenty years, cleared his throat again.

"Doctor?"

Gerald raised his head and stared at the detective; his brow furrowed in confusion.

"I beg your pardon?"

"I asked if you could give me a description of the men who did this."

"Yes, I'm sorry. I, uh, there were four of them. All appeared around your age, scruffy, like those thugs from the movies about motorcycle gangs."

"I'm afraid there is a lot of gang activity in this area, some kind of rogue motorcycle group. Most of those guys are harmless, just bike enthusiasts, you know what I mean?"

The doctor stared at the detective, and the man rubbed a hand across his cheek.

"No, I suppose you don't. What were you doing in that alley anyway?"

"Are you insinuating this is our fault?"

"Of course not. It's just I--"

"You assume a couple of old fuddy duddies don't understand the 'real world' and just walk around as if life is just a bed of roses."

"That's not what I meant."

"No, you only mean to help, don't you, detective? To what end? We both know you'll never catch them and even if you do, I'm sure there will be little to no evidence of their guilt."

"Please, sir, I'm sorry. If you could just give a statement-"

"Oh, I'll tell you everything. But don't think for one minute that I'll be waiting around for the police to bring those…those murderers to justice."

Gerald played the interview over in his head as he sat in his living room. He gave the police the whole story from the short walk from the theater to their car, to the final blow that took Emily's life, and every horrible act in between. He had no faith in the police, in society, or the law to make this wrong right.

But he had faith in himself.

The former warmth and inviting atmosphere of their home lay quiet and hollow. Emily's absence made it less somehow, smaller, insignificant. He stared down at his hands, the palms still raw with scrapes from when the men had first knocked him down. His and Emily's dried blood stiffened the cuffs of his dress shirt.

Emily.

Fresh tears spilled onto his hands, stinging the raw wounds. He clenched his fists, squeezing blood onto the thick pile of the beige carpet. He moved his hands back and forth, creating the shape of a question mark onto the floor. What would he to do now? What was his next move? How could he go on without Emily by his side?

Dr. Farrow.

The name popped into his head. An old colleague, Gerald had neither seen nor thought of Farrow in years, not since the man moved to Europe a decade ago. Though they'd gone in different directions academically - he into chemistry and Farrow anthropology - they'd always remained close friends, each trying to outdo the other comparing the difficulties of their fields.

Surely Farrow would have an answer. Studying dozens of culture's histories, politics, mythologies, and rituals, Farrow must have come across information that could help Gerald with what he had in mind.

Part of him recognized, if only for the briefest of moments, that he'd cracked from grief. What he was even considering, let alone already beginning to plan, would assure him a one-way admittance into Walter Reuther Psych. He didn't care. Life without Emily would be unbearable. He had to do something.

Within a month, Gerald sat in Farrow's home as they sipped tea and stared out at the deep blue water below. Farrow stared at his friend over the delicate China cup, his bushy eyebrows raised in shock.

"You can't be serious."

"Oh I most assuredly am, my friend."

"Resurrection."

"Yes."

"Emily's resurrection."

"Naturally."

"And you've come to me because…?"

Gerald stared at his friend. Farrow's lips curled up into a lopsided grin.

"All right, yes. I've encountered many a belief and custom across multiple cultures when it comes to black magic."

"I'm not talking magic, Farrow. That implies make-believe."

"Fine, fine. I understand what you're getting at. But you don't honestly believe any of them can be real, do you?"

"I do, and I intend to prove it."

Farrow sighed and put his cup on the table. "Look, Gerald. I understand what you're going through."

"No, you don't."

"Touché. Even so, this is not the path for you to follow. It's not real."

"It is. It has to be. I'll find it but I need your help."

"I won't do it. I will not help you literally dive headfirst into this black pool of madness, Gerald."

Farrow pushed his chair back from the table and turned to walk away from the conversation. Gerald lurched forward, grabbing his friend by the arm.

"You have to help me, Richard. You have to."

Gerald fell to his knees, weeping and sobbing like a child.

"I beg you. You have to help me find it. You think I've gone mad. I haven't. But I surely will if I have to live one more second, drowning in the hopelessness that has threatened to overcome me since the moment

Emily took her last breath."

Farrow stood over his long-time friend. His heart broke with Gerald's every cry, every hitch that rocked his body. He knelt down and laid a hand on the man's shoulder.

"All right, my friend. All right. I'll help you. God forgive me, I'll help you."

Two years of dusty libraries, archeological digs, historical site visits, eating questionable dishes and draining half his savings to "get in good with the locals" just to find any small snippet of information on resurrection rites. But eventually it paid off. Musty books, ancient carvings, oral histories and more all contained the same nugget of information regarding one ingredient key to every ritual he'd found: Gorgon blood.

Euryale and Stheno sat at a small table at an outdoor cafe. The week of scorching temperatures had broken after a heavy rainstorm. The cool damp air reminded them both of the summers they'd lived back home in Greece centuries before.

"Who knew Podunk, Michigan would have such a similar climate to Corfu."

"Stheno, why must you speak with such vulgarities?"

"It's Stef now. And you gotta get with the times. We walk around talking the way you do-"

"You mean properly?"

"Like you've got a giant two by four jammed up your ass, and people will start looking at you funny. And when people start doing that, they notice how different you are."

Euryale nodded. "And when they notice those differences, they get scared."

"And out come the pitchforks."

"I know, I do. It is just so distasteful."

"I know we haven't seen each other in decades but we're together again. I'll help ease you into the 21st century as painless as possible. Whaddya say?"

"I suppose I have little choice in the matter."

"Exactly. And no time like the present. That guy over there has been staring at you for the past ten minutes."

Euryale turned to look but Stef gripped her arm.

"Don't look, Lee. We don't want to be obvious."

"Oh, in the name of Anthena's little owl. Please do not call me--"

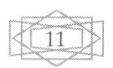

"Damn, he's coming over. Act natural."

"Is that not the precise opposite of what you want me to do?"

"Shush."

"Excuse me, ladies. I'm sorry to interrupt."

Stef smiled at him. "No sorry necessary. What can we do for you?"

The man nodded at Stef but turned his full attention to Euryale.

"May I sit?"

Euryale looked up at the human. Small in stature, middle aged or older, someone she could snap easily in two if necessary. Not a threat.

"If you must."

"Lee," Stef hissed at her sister. She covered the faux pas with a laugh and gestured for the man to take her seat.

"Please, sit. I was just leaving anyway."

"Where are you going?" Euryale clenched her jaw to refrain from showing panic. Though this human may be of little concern, she didn't need to display any weakness in front of him.

"Don't worry about me, Lee. Please, enjoy…"

"Oh, uh Ionian. Dr. Harvey Ionian."

"Enjoy Doctor Ionian's company for a while. I'll call you later."

"Call me what?"

Stef waved goodbye and practically skipped down the sidewalk. She glanced over her shoulder at Euryale, offering a wink and a wave, before disappearing around the nearest corner. Euryale wanted to run after her but the man cleared his throat and she turned her attention back to him.

"Are you sure I'm not interrupting?" he asked.

"You will have to forgive her, doctor. She and I do not share the same ideas when it comes to societal niceties."

His mouth split into a wide grin and to her surprise, Euryale found herself mirroring his expression.

"Why do you smile so?"

"Forgive me. I'm not laughing at you or anything so rude. I just haven't heard anyone speak so well since my wife passed. So many youngsters today with their slang and mutilated grammar."

"Oh, if only my sister had remained. It would be good for her to hear such words. She is like a nagging elder the way she scolds me about my speech."

The doctor's eye widened in surprise and he coughed. "Your sister?"

Euryale nodded. "Older one at that. Sometimes she acts younger than her years."

"Ah, yes. My older brother used to be the same way. Always called me an old fuddy duddy, even in our youth."

They shared a laugh and Euryale realized she enjoyed Ionian's company. She hadn't opened herself up to any interactions with humans for decades. Perhaps building a new friendship would be good for her, one she could enjoy for years to come.

These Things Move in Cycles

by M.C. St. John

It starts with an egg floating in the deep.
The egg is a small gelatinous sac, no bigger than the motes of silt and industrial plastic that twist with the ebb and surge of the sea. The egg rides the current through milky shafts of light. It slips through tendrils of kelp, navigates skeletons of sunken ships. The waters are cold, unrelenting. But the egg flashes green-gold in the gloom, its nucleus of cells eager but patient.
The sound of the freighter precedes the actual ship. The thrumming propellors churn up the water. The USS Aurora is sailing along its trade route. It is packed to the gills with goods for American consumers: imported liquor and beer, sneakers, fireworks, sex toys, and the like. Demand for instant gratification is high. The free market is more than happy to fulfill its promise by any means necessary.
Take the ship itself. Though weighted down by its capitalistic bounty, the USS Aurora is making up for lost time to customers by doubling its speed. Metric tons of crude oil burn at an alarming rate inside its fuel tanks, some of which spews into the open water. In the USS Aurora's wake is a shimmering trail of beautiful yet toxic pollution that perversely lives up to the ship's namesake.
The stern splits the sea into choppy chevrons. The egg roils around the starboard side and crests a wave with a spray of seawater. It is momentarily lost in the confusion before appearing again, unscathed.
Through an act of serendipity and environmental neglect, the USS Aurora has not been properly cleaned. Alongside the barnacles and rust on its hull are clusters of zebra mussels, a highly invasive species. The egg finds refuge within the shell of one of these mussels.
Time passes in fits and starts. On a primordial level, the egg senses the change in scenery. It has doubled in size, now as large as a green cat's-eye marble. Originally, it was tight quarters inside the shell. But after eating the mussel—absorbing the tender flesh into its own—the egg

has had room to grow. Light and shadow move across the slit opening of its newfound home. For now, it watches and waits.

The USS Aurora makes its way through the northern channels between Canada and America, navigating the lock system in Sault St. Marie, where the freighter rises to meet Lake Superior. And although the egg had grown accustomed to the salt and cold of previous waters, it can adapt. It has before.

When the USS Aurora docks and releases its bilge water into the harbor, the egg seizes the opportunity. As the fetid water washes over the hull, the egg slips from its shell and plops into the harbor.

There are many ships coming and going in Sault St. Marie, both commercial and private. Of the latter is a high-end speedboat owned by Bud Larson, a retired accidents-claim lawyer from Chicago. While in Sault St. Marie, Bud has spent his time on his speedboat fishing, where he caught little, and cruising along the shoreline for a future ex-wife, where he caught none.

Fortunately for him, Bud has also bought a retirement home in the Upper Peninsula. His lounge there is stocked with his favorite liquor, an imported brand that the USS Aurora counted as its cargo. He decides to go home to drink and brood. He heads to a nearby launch, hitches up his speedboat, and drives out into the gathering summer dusk.

What Bud Larson does not know is that he has picked up a hitchhiker.

It is not as if Bud would have noticed. The creature blends in with the pale green fiberglass of the speedboat. Still, we must give Bud some credit: the creature would have been hard for a trained biologist to identify, let alone a bitter, lovelorn lawyer.

The creature would have difficulty recognizing itself. It has come a long way from the innocent egg it once was. After diving into the harbor, it clung to a kelp-covered dock post. Small schools of minnows passed by it. Eventually, a curious minnow got too close. More made the same mistake.

With each of its meals, the egg grew. Its cells multiplied. Its body elongated. Flippers tipped with claws sprouted from its sides. A tail grew at one end. A head emerged from the other. One with thick, fleshy lips and sharp teeth.

The creature also developed an acute sense of smell. While clinging to the speedboat Bud Larson pulls down a dark county road, the creature inhales the warm aromas of pine sap and asphalt, punctuated by tasty hints of roadkill. It discerns that this world is yet another sea full of prey.

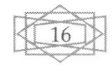

Although it is hungry, it is still unsure how to eat anything in this new, drier place. Everything is so bright, so loud. The noise is enough to rupture its soft skull. Luckily, it catches a whiff of something familiar that distracts it from the barrage of sound. It skitters into the speedboat to investigate.

Lodged between the captain's chair and steering console is a styrofoam cooler tied with yellow nylon rope. During the bumpy drive, the cooler's lid loosened. The smell of cold lake water wafts out. The creature sniffs again, then bites through the nylon rope. The lid flies off into the night.

Inside the cooler, lying in a slush of ice, are the few fish Bud Larson managed to catch. They are Asian carp, which, like the zebra mussels, are another invasive species for the Great Lakes. In recent years, the carp have been rebranded as copi to change public opinion (and stomachs) about eating these interlopers. Regardless of the name, the animals are still a threat to the ecological balance. If left uncaught and unchecked, the copi would fill the lakes and choke out the native wildlife.

Bud Larson is largely clueless about this existential struggle when he was fishing. Like most invasive predators, he will eat what he can catch until his dying breath. The adolescent creature aboard his speedboat possesses the same instinct. With a quiver of hungry delight, it dives into the cooler. Icy water splashes up. Soon the water is stained pink, flecked with fish scales and bits of styrofoam.

Meanwhile, Bud Larson, oblivious, drives with his radio tuned to an oldies station. Eddie Money sings "Two Tickets to Paradise," and Bud plays percussion on the steering wheel, his thoughts fixed on his lounge and a tumbler of scotch.

North of Marquette lies the small town of Devonia, Michigan, where Bud has bought his retirement home. He drives past the estuary that bears the town's name, in reference to the age of prehistoric fossils that were discovered along its banks. The river is low and sluggish that feeds the Devonia estuary, moving fast enough to avoid stagnation. From the road, the waters appear brackish and otherworldly. Ancient trees jut from the water's surface, the branches reaching for the half-moon above. The estuary looks more like a swamp, or even a lagoon. Smells like one too.

The creature draws a deep breath, closing its eyes in rapture. Yes, it thinks with a rapidly developing brain. Warm. Food. Home. Go.

As Bud Larson slows for a curve, the creature leaps from the speedboat.

Since its feast of copi, the creature has developed thicker forearms with stronger clawed flippers. With them, the creature lands softly on the gravel at the side of the road. Gone is its soft, wet whip of a tail; in its place is a pair of nascent legs, thin and spindly as a young bullfrog's. On the road, the creature forces itself to use those new back legs, moving in a series of awkward hop-steps. Each time those legs pump, they grow stronger, the muscles rippling. Before the creature reaches the shoreline, it scuttles on all four of its limbs quite well.

The Devonia estuary serves as home for many fish, foul, and amphibians. At the height of June, temperatures are pleasant in northern Michigan, the optimal conditions for these species. However, climate change has ravaged that status quo. This summer has been unseasonably sticky. Algae has bloomed faster in the low-lying waters, cutting off sunlight and delaying breeding for many animals. A film the color and consistency of snot has settled on the waters, covering all matter of activity below the surface.

Though this change in season is terrible for the original denizens—those that have evolved with the landscape for millennia—it is paradise for a well-adapted newcomer. The creature is a fast learner.

Over the next few weeks, the estuary grows unusually quiet. The trilling of frogs goes first. The lonely morning warbles of loons is cut short. Even the rutting call of a young male moose rises to hysterics before being silenced in rippling rings of green water. This is not to mention the quiet creatures in the waters themselves—the trout, blue gill, salmon, and, yes, copi. They too go, albeit quietly. A burble of water, a flip of a fin, then a slow trail of bubbles.

Nobody in town is aware that the estuary has turned into a feeding ground. Certainly not Tommy Barnes and Magda Sinclair, soon-to-be juniors at Devonia High when school starts up again in the fall.

This summer night, the couple is only interested in finding a nice place to make out that is not the driveway to Magda's house, where her stepdad Carl can totally watch them from the upstairs bedroom. Can we say creeper much? For sure.

But Magda also has to admit that it is Carl's job to, like, look after her. It was Magda and her mom for the longest time; then it was them plus Carl, until her mom got sick. Things have been hard now that it's been just Carl and Magda.

What complicates things is that Carl is the sheriff of Devonia. He looks over the four-hundred-odd people in town and tries to keep an eye on Magda. Though nothing really happens in Devonia outside of a drunk and disorderly at the Moosejaw Tavern, Sheriff Carl is the guy who deals with things when things go sideways. But it has been his new role as single stepdad that's been the real struggle, finding the right balance between work and family.

For example, Carl doesn't trust Tommy Barnes, and not just because Tommy is dating Magda. Carl has known the Barnes family through his policework. Many of those drunken escapades at the Moosejaw Tavern involved a Barnes or two. They usually devolved into brawls over a woman. Carl and his deputies had to haul several Barnes boys to the station on the grounds of jaded love.

Yet Magda protested that Tommy was different than his jerk uncles and cousins and brothers Carl has had to contend with over the years. Tommy was sensitive. Carl had his doubts. In his view, genes had a curious way of expressing themselves in a family line. Each Barnes was different, yes, but each Barnes was the same old animal. It was a matter of knowing when they'd turn.

Tonight at the estuary is such a test. Watch the headlights of Tommy Barnes's old pickup sweep across the mossy water. See how they throw shadows from the half-submerged trees like long, clawed hands. Then the lights go out, the engine dies. The only light is the full moon peeking through a scud of clouds. It illuminates the couple in the truck bed, where Tommy has thrown down a light wool blanket to cover the rough patches as best he can.

Some canoodling commences.

Magda Sinclair enjoys it at first, the heat and the rush of things. She too is an animal, and not above the pleasure of sexual instinct, so long as it is her own to relish. That is, until she does not enjoy herself, and voices her opinion.

Tommy does not take well to what he perceives as criticism. Why does she have to be such a rule follower? Can't she ever just let loose? Sheriff Carl is her stepdad, for chrissakes—what's he gonna do, arrest her for going all the way?

Magda hates Tommy's accusations. They not only ruin the mood for tonight but also support the totally annoying fact that maybe Carl was right. Either way, she wants to go home. They are, like, done here.

Tommy is not happy. In fact, he's downright pissed, and says as much, along with several curse words aimed at Magda and Sheriff Carl. Tommy's voice carries across the estuary farther than usual. Without the ambient noise from regular critters, the boy is easily the loudest thing for a quarter mile in any direction.

As if he is thinking of the surrounding environment. Standing in the truck bed and hollering, Tommy Barnes has turned his back on the scuzzy estuary waters not out of spite so much as entrenched superiority. He is the dominant party here. He is the alpha in this situation. What could possibly upset this natural order?

Magda Sinclair discovers the answer. She never wished for it, at least not like this. But rarely do these hard truths come with pretense or warning.

The creature appears as swiftly as a nightmare. One moment it is part of the shadow of a sunken tree; the next moment it has leaped from the waters to the shore. It now carries itself with poise and balance. Those once-fragile legs have strengthened with each successful hunt.

So has the rest of its body. Standing in the moonlight, the creature is now six feet of rough green muscle. Fine rills striate its features. Streams of water sluice from these rills, much like the bilge water from the USS Aurora, and for a similar purpose: they help the creature cut through water to catch prey without detection.

Magda is not thinking about the evolutionary advantages of swimming rills. Her mind is riddled with adrenaline. She lies in the truck bed, tangled in the wool blanket and staring at the creature that has appeared at the back bumper. What she notices first are its eyes, like bright coins in the grotto of its face. Those eyes fix themselves on Magda. She grows cold under their curious gaze. This thing is interested in her, which is the last thing she wants, like, ever.

Tommy continues with his rant.

"Why are all girls like this? You all are so damned emotional that you don't know how to function. Why don't you say what you mean and do what you say and make a decision for once in your—"

Tommy doesn't finish. That last word escapes him. It is replaced with an inarticulate yowl as the creature grabs his belt, the limp buckle dangling from his half-buttoned jeans. The clawed flippers dig in and then yank. Tommy, still yowling, is lifted high into the air.

The creature's green-gold eyes flick back to Magda, who sits stunned.

What does that look mean from this thing? Magda has a sinking feeling it might be you're next. But why does she not fully believe that's the case?

Because there is a mixture of emotions on the face of this creature that Magda recognizes. It reminds her of Carl. Dumb, overbearing, and only-sometimes-fun Carl. Magda would see similar emotions on her stepdad's face when she came home late without calling or when, at the fever pitch of an argument, she would claim she was not, like, his real daughter anyway. Carl would flinch with a blend of affection and anger, exasperation and sadness. A guardian's love, devotion tried to its breaking point. Magda marvels at the resemblance in this creature's face.

Then the moment passes when Tommy, in his frantic writhing, conks the creature with the heel of a boot.

The creature blinks in pain. An angry hiss escapes its lips. The rills along its body ripple in annoyance. The creature seems to remember again what it was doing. Intruder, it reminds itself. Threat. It then crouches down on those strong back legs and launches Tommy Barnes over a copse of cattails. There's a splash and a thud and Tommy—for the time being or longer—is silent.

The creature turns back to the sound of the pickup's engine. Magda is behind the wheel, her cellphone tossed into a cupholder. Out of instinct, she has already texted Carl the most pressing information (ezstuary / soutth side& / T hurt / MONSTERR) and is ready to hit the road into town. She said what she meant, and she was going to do what she said.

She can make decisions. She can take care of business.

Magda drops the truck into gear, hits the gas. The spinning tires fling gravel and mud. The creature raises a flipper to protect itself. The truck fishtails, the back tires searching for a grip in the soft earth. The creature lunges closer to the truck, intent on puncturing a tire to still the loud machine. Anything to keep the waters quiet and still. It has worked so hard to escape the noises of this strange, dry world and make this estuary its proper home.

But as the creature prepares to swipe, Magda punches the accelerator and wrenches the steering wheel. The truck swings wildly. The back bumper nails the creature. It is the equivalent of backing into a tree trunk, the hard shudder and thrust against a stubborn object. The collision pops the back tires from their muddy ruts. The truck catches stable ground.

Magda doesn't wait.

The truck hurtles up the trail to the country road. There's a dip in the shoulder along the curve, the very one that Bud Larson had to slow down for several weeks ago. Magda hits it head-on. The truck's cab bounces down first, the suspension rattling, followed by the bed, which thumps even harder.

Magda straightens out the truck as best she can. It's hard to gain speed. The back bumper is dragging. She checks the gear shift. She's not in neutral but drive, so what gives?

Meanwhile, her cellphone lights up. She had managed to take the thing off silent. The ringtone she's set for Carl fills the cab: "Two Tickets to Paradise" by Eddie Money. She thought it was hilarious when she had programmed it for her stepdad (cheesy tune for a cheesy dude). Now, though? It plays like a soundtrack to a bad dream.

Magda fumbles to turn off the cellphone while still holding onto the wheel. When she looks up, she catches sight of something in the rearview mirror.

Illuminated by the cellphone light is the creature.

It is crouched in the truck bed. That thing was what was weighing down the back end. And now it is reaching in through the back window like Magda had when she slipped into the cab to start the engine. The creature is much larger than she is, so it has managed only to slip one arm through. The thick smells of algae and rank fish arrive with it. Magda gags, then ducks her head. The clawed flipper swipes through the headrest and eviscerates the upholstery. Too close, too close…

This was not how this night was supposed to go.

Ever since she lost her mom, Magda has thought a lot about life and death. How her mom's decisions brought Magda into this world, and how those choices carried the two of them to Devonia, to Carl, and, ultimately, to her mom's sickness. It was a crazy, zigzagging line, a spider's web of cause and effect. Through the hard times, Magda felt like the victim of circumstance. Since her mom's funeral, she had wanted to break free, chart her own path. It was why dating Tommy felt like freedom. It was a chance at free will.

But now? Now Magda's decisions feel like a repeat performance of her mom's, a strange variation that leads to the same tragic end. Is this what life was all about? Trying and failing to love, to survive, over and over, until something eats you up? If that was the case, Magda thinks it's a cruel game.

Except here's the thing: she doesn't pull over and quit. She keeps driving. Even with a literal lake creature latched onto the truck cab ready to tear her to bits, she pushes on. That will to live is also reminiscent of Magda's mom, who fought to the very end, even in hospice. If she was going down, it would be on her own terms. Magda would do the same.

When another light flashes across her vision, Magda braces herself for Eddie Money's offer for tickets to paradise. It doesn't come, much to her relief. These lights are not from Magda's cellphone but out on the road. Headlights. They are leaving town, rounding south on the curve of the estuary, heading toward Magda.

The first set of headlights belongs to Sheriff Carl's police cruiser.

After having read Magda's misspelled texts, Carl hightailed it to the estuary. Despite many moody misgivings from her stepdaughter, Magda was never one to get sloppy with her texting, especially to Carl. The content of the jumbled message was bad enough (T hurt), but the frantic execution struck a chord of fear in him (MONSTERR).

In a terrible coincidence, Carl had been called in to the Moosejaw Tavern to break up a fight between some locals and—you guessed it—several of the Barnes boys. This time, two of Tommy's brothers, one of his uncles, and his own father were involved. While Carl's deputies calmed down things, Carl had received Magda's messages. Without thinking, he told them Tommy was hurt and Magda was in danger before running to his cruiser.

On the road behind Carl, then, are three more sets of headlights: two trucks full of keyed-up Barneses followed by a Devonia deputy cruiser.

Carl disregards whatever is trailing behind him. He is only looking to what's ahead. His headlights pick up Tommy Barnes's truck, with Magda behind the wheel. Carl's heart triphammers when he sees his stepdaughter isn't alone.

Crouched on the roof of the cab is a creature.

To Carl, the thing looks like some reject from a monster movie. The problem is that there is no zipper to this costume. This thing is a wild animal, a real monster. Magda was not exaggerating. Now this monster is taking its claws to the truck's windshield. The glass spiderwebs with every blow. And if it gets in…

Carl hits his police siren, which shrieks into the night.

It's the first thing that pops into his mind to do, and it's a good move. The creature flicks up its head to stare at the cruiser. Its thick lips pull back into a sneer, revealing sharp, glistening teeth. But its eyes are scrunched in pain. The noise of the siren is too much, and it wobbles on the roof, unsure of its balance.

What doesn't help is that the truck itself is wobbling too.

With no visible windshield to see through, Magda struggles to keep the truck on the road. She hears the siren and knows it's Carl. Her lame, reliable stepdad has come to the rescue. Instead of thanking him by running directly into his cruiser, Magda straightens her wheel and lets her foot off the gas. The truck had been hugging the curve around the estuary. Now the truck skids off the road—missing Carl's cruiser by a half a dozen yards—and lands in a marshy ditch.

The next few moments happen fast.

Carl cuts his siren, parks the cruiser, runs for the truck. Magda kicks open the truck door and sprints up the embankment. They meet on the white line marking the curve of the road and embrace.

The Barneses' trucks also screech to a halt. Each angry, tipsy relation leaps out; each one has pulled either a handgun from the glovebox or a hunting rifle from the rack. They too saw that crazy thing on Tommy's ride. If that monster hurt their boy, they were going to return the favor and then some.

And the creature does appear. Though it had been thrown from the truck into the underbrush, been battered and bruised, it can't escape its own instincts. It rears up out of the ditch, covered in mud and dirty water. It must cross the road and dive back into the estuary, back to the home it had made for itself.

It lurches into the glow of the crossing headlights. It casts long, jagged shadows in many directions. In that one moment, the creature is a tableau of terror fit for a midnight movie poster.

Then the Barnes boys open fire.

It doesn't last long. Extermination of a wild animal never does at point-blank range. But this creature, limping and bleeding ichor, succeeds in collapsing into the estuary. It splashes into the thick green water and dives, or sinks, below the surface and disappears. Though Tommy's dad is the last to fire his handgun into the water, it's more out of blind anger than accuracy. Carl's deputies command the Barnes boys to drop their weapons. Unbelievably, the Barnes comply with the authorities for once. The melee is over.

Everyone stands and watches the estuary in the moonlight.

Nothing moves. All is quiet.

It stays that way even after they all head back to town.

Tommy Barnes, concussed from his fall in the cattails but very much alive, is in tow in his dad's truck. Magda does not ride with him. She rides with Carl instead, insists on it, in fact. She has decided things are over for her and Tommy. Magda knows that Carl doesn't like Tommy. But Magda also knows her mom wouldn't like him either. That decides things in Magda's mind, once and for all.

Some things run their course and are done. What seems like it could last forever is really a passing phase. And that's okay. So long as you can accept the changes, big or small, as they come, you can learn to survive.

A few days later, it is the Fourth of July. Like most small towns in America, Devonia is no stranger to the celebration of independence. As dusk settles again over Lake Superior, locals along the shoreline set off loads of fireworks, many of which, incidentally, came from the haul brought in by the USS Aurora. No matter where they come from, the colorful explosions in the sky are a sight to see reflected in the deep, dark waters of a Great Lake.

Out on the dock of his retirement home, Bud Larson tips his tumbler of scotch skyward. He may be alone, but he's got a piece of heaven up here, so that counts for something. However, he did have to order a pizza instead of frying up his copi. He may be the first guy to lose his fish after he had them in the cooler. Still, there's always next week to go out and try again.

Tommy Barnes shares the same sentiment. Though Magda broke it off with him, he is more than okay with not dating the sheriff's kid. There will plenty of other girls to date when junior year starts. He still doesn't quite remember what happened between his argument with Magda and waking up on a soggy log in the estuary. That's also for the best, he thinks. The family that came out to rescue him have been drinking more than usual and whispering about what they thought they saw. Sometimes, Tommy figures, it's better not to ask about things you don't want to know. Better to watch the fireworks and forget.

The feeling couldn't be more different for Magda Sinclair. If anything, she will always remember that night, starting with those golden eyes in the dark. She isn't afraid to remember, though. Truth be told, she wants to hold on to that sharp, clear drive to live as long as she can. Her mom would want that for her. Sitting in an Adirondack chair on the front lawn, marveling at the blues and reds and greens blossoming above her, Magda wants nothing more than to stay in this moment.

Next to her in a matching Adirondack chair is Sheriff Carl, who is simply Carl this Fourth for once. Carl has taken the holiday for him and Magda, leaving his deputies in charge. He understands he can't protect Devonia from everything all the time, but he can allow himself a day off every now and then. Magda will be a junior this fall, one year closer to graduation and eventually college, likely out-of-state. He didn't plan on becoming a dad, but now that he is, he is just now understanding the fierce love he harbors for his kid. He would do anything for Magda, including letting her go when she's ready to leave.

The fireworks also light up the Devonia estuary, where most of the wildlife had already left. However, there are signs that even that is not permanent. A few frogs have begun trilling in the cattails. Herons stalk around the shoreline, calling out to mates. The major predator has left the area. The animals have taken notice and made tentative returns. It will never be the same as it once was, but some new balance will arrive soon enough. All it takes is time.

At this hour, the estuary waters are flowing outward to Lake Superior. Beneath the algae, a dark body stirs from the river bottom. The creature, once so strong and deadly, tumbles along with the current, another casualty of the moving tide. It had tried to adapt to a new world and failed for itself.

But for the time it was here, the creature had made a good home. It kept the estuary quiet and warm and dark. It provided as much food as it could muster, protected against predators until the very end. For following these instincts, the creature did succeed.

The nest it had built survived.

It ends with a mother's body bumping against her clutch of eggs, small gelatinous sacs no bigger than motes of algae. They briefly appear as an underwater firework, those sparks of life dispersing every which way and riding the currents to parts unknown.

Some will fall into the silt and be buried; others will be gobbled up by fish, possibly copi; still more may be lost in the dark waters.

But one will find a home.

When the time is right, one always does.

An Eye for Beauty

by R D Doan

    Let me tell you what I've learned from this whole ordeal. Sometimes, it's best to let beauty be experienced rather than be captured.

    I know how that sounds, coming from somebody who practically grew up behind the camera looking for that prized winning shot, but trust me, no matter how good you think you are, or how good you actually are, there will be a moment or two that will stop you from taking a shot. Instead of trying to capture that perfect moment, perfect scene or essence of someone, you'll put down that camera and just enjoy the view instead. Or, if you're like me, you won't but wish you did. Oh, how I wish I would have listened to my gut and walked away.

    We're all driven by something, aren't we? Money, fame, success, validation. I wanted to be the very best, and Dorian? Well, he just wanted a photo to last forever. But it's like I said, sometimes, it's best to let beauty be experienced rather than be captured.

    I've been taking pictures for as long as I can remember. When I was a little, I was the flower girl for my Uncle Charlie's wedding. Naturally, I had my picture taken a lot, and I wanted to know how that little black box could capture a moment and freeze it forever, with just a click of a button! The hired photographer showed me how the camera worked, and I was hooked. For my tenth birthday, my parents gave me a Polaroid camera; you know, one of those cameras that spits out a self-developing square photo right after you take it? I loved that camera. If I'm being honest, what I really loved about the camera was the satisfaction of seeing what I captured in the photo that came after. I took maybe a million pictures. Okay, probably not a million, but it sure felt like it when I was ten. I took so many pictures because I could never seem to capture what I saw through the view finder. All the pictures looked static. They lacked something. So, I kept trying. I kept taking pictures.

    After spending a small fortune on film for my Polaroid camera, my parents thought it better to buy me a digital camera instead. They succeeded in saving money, but inadvertently fueled my passion for photography by giving me an essentially endless roll of film. With the ability to take as many pictures as I wanted, my desire to capture that perfect photo became an obsession. I began to experiment with things like lighting and exposure, and in the process, I became more artistic and expressive. As my photography skills evolved, my parents saw my potential and supported my dream to be a professional photographer.

Like any other artist, I wanted to be the best. I wanted to push past what everyone else was doing and finally be able to show in pictures what apparently only I could see. I wanted to show the beauty and life that radiated from everything. The only trouble was I still couldn't quite capture it the way I saw it. I was missing something. I needed to learn the trade and break through whatever was holding me back. I decided to enroll at GVSU in Grand Rapids, MI to learn a bit more and hone my skills.

In Grand Rapids, I had anonymity. Nobody knew my work, nobody held me on a pedestal, and nobody cared. The city was full of life and I had to fight the urge to take pictures of everything and everyone. I could practically see the glow of life bleeding out of every crack, every crevice, and every building I passed on the streets. I could see life beaming from faces on the homeless and from the strangers sitting on the buses. Life was everywhere around me and nobody seemed to take notice.

My classes didn't offer me much instruction or enjoyment initially. The instructors were teaching techniques I had already mastered on my own. I was getting increasingly bored of my classes and would find myself frequently skipping class to take photos in the city parks. It was on one such occasion, at Lacks Park near the Blue Bridge, I met the man who provided the missing link to something I was beginning to believe wasn't possible.

I was lying in the grass under a tree taking pictures, trying to capture the sunlight shining through yellowed leaves, when a dark shadowy figure obstructed my view. Through my viewfinder, I saw a frightening silhouette of a man outlined by brilliant light standing over me. I moved my camera to see who could be so rude and was left speechless. Standing over me was the most beautiful man I'd ever seen.

He turned and looked up to the tree branches above us and back to me and said, "Tell me, what do you see?"

I couldn't think of anything to say, and quite honestly, if I had said anything at all, I'm sure it would have been something embarrassing or incoherent.

He sat down next to me, gestured to my camera, and looked up to the tree branches again.

"It's beautiful isn't it?" he asked.

"Yes," I said, finally able to find my voice. "I love the way the light shines through the fall colors. It gives the impression of life bursting from each leaf."

The man nodded. "Why not take pictures of the bridge? It seems to be a pretty popular among tourists."

To emphasize his point, he gestured to the crowd of people taking photos of the bridge with the rising cityscape behind it. It was common subject matter for my classmates with the park's close proximity to the downtown campus.

I shrugged. "I don't know; it's been done. I mean, it just seems too…uninteresting?"

"I agree. You certainly have an eye for beauty," the man said. "I'm Dorian. It's a pleasure to meet someone with similar artistic taste."

"Sibyl. It's nice to meet you."

Dorian and I sat in the shade of the tree and discussed how we both had come to West Michigan. I told him about my photography and how I was enrolled at GVSU to fine tune my skills. He told me he was in the city for a few months to check out the museums and galleries while he searched for up-and-coming artists.

"A painting can be breathtakingly beautiful if done well, but like the beauty it captures, it too fades over time. The paint can slowly decay. It can dry up, crack, or wilt under the presence of time," he said. "Sadly, a painting won't last forever."

His eyes were mesmerizing. I hung on every word he said.

"I've had several paintings over the years that were so magnificent you'd think their artists had made a deal with the devil to make them so good. But they too will tarnish over time." He reached out and took my hands in his. "Do you know what I like about photographs?"

I shook my head. He was touching my hands. My heart was racing.

"They last forever. Well, digital photos do. I suppose printed photos fade with time too, but digital photos will live on forever," Dorian said with a gleam in his eyes.

"Just imagine. If you took a portrait with a digital camera, the original would stay vibrant and viable for all of eternity. It'd be immortal!"

"You mean if pictures were living things, then they'd be immortal," I said. "Pictures are just pictures. They can only capture a moment in life.

They aren't alive. Mortality or immortality only applies to living things. But I get what you're trying to say. The picture will out-live us all," I said, with "live" in air quotes.

"Do you only take nature and landscape pictures? Or do you take portraits as well?" he asked, changing the subject.

"I've been known to do both," I replied.

Dorian and I walked for what must have been several hours by the time we found ourselves approaching the Amway Grand Hotel. We passed the time chatting about life in the city and our mutual love for the arts. It wasn't hard to get lost in conversation with Dorian. He was a great listener, very charming, and easy on the eyes.

He seemed interested and engaged when I spoke about life in the city, but when the conversation shifted to my photography, he practically lit up with excitement. He asked the usual, basic questions, like what medium I preferred to work in; digital photography, of course. He asked if I had a favorite camera. I said I preferred my Nikon Z50. He eventually evolved to deeper questions, like what images I hoped to capture. He asked what feelings I hoped to conjure with my work.

"Back at the park, I could tell you were different from the others. You saw something in the tree branches and leaves that the others couldn't. What did you see?"

"I don't know if I can explain it," I said.

Dorian grabbed my hand and pulled me to a stop. We had circled all the way back to Fulton Street, across the river from Lacks park, where we first met.

"Please try. I'm dying to know," he replied.

I nodded and sighed.

"Okay, so when I look at something, I can easily see that there's a natural beauty about it. You know? I mean, everything can be beautiful, right? Beauty is in the eye of the beholder, and all that. But, when I look at the same thing through my camera, I can actually see the beauty within. And it doesn't seem to matter if I use a fancy camera like this Nikon or if it's a throwaway film camera or a Polaroid, it's always the same. I see this light that seems to burst from the object or person. It's crazy, or I'm crazy, or... you probably think I'm crazy," I said, blushing as I looked to my feet.

Dorian lifted my chin with his hand and shook his head.

"No. You're not crazy. I don't think you're crazy. I promise," he said. "Have you been able to capture what you see on film?"

"No, I mean, I was close once. Just before I left for GVSU, my dog Peaches had gotten pretty sick. He was pretty old, and he'd been with me for all my awkward teen years. He was pretty special to me. So, when he got sick the week before I moved to Grand Rapids, and didn't look like he'd pull through, I was devastated. All I wanted was a photo of him before he passed. A few days before my move, I saw him peacefully napping in the sunlight by our back door. He was curled up with his nose tucked into his hind legs and looked so peaceful. When I looked at him through the camera, the familiar "life glow" was there. With tears in my eyes, I snapped what I believed would be the last photo of Peaches. Then, to my absolute amazement, the resulting photo had a radiate glow around the sleeping dog. It was the only time I had successfully captured the glow, and I had no idea how I'd done it."

"I have a theory, but to fully explain it, I'll need to show you something," Dorian said. He took me by the hand and led me over the Blue Bridge.

The park was littered with people enjoying the unseasonably warm weather. When we entered the park, the sun was setting on the city skyline and the streetlamps along the paved paths were just turning on. The effect was beautiful. Dorian led me down the paved path under the bridge.

"It's beautiful and so full of life. Do you see it?" he asked.

I did, actually. The underside of the bridge was mundane, and yet it was beautiful in its own way. I took aim with my camera and found the familiar beaming light shining through and nodded.

"Of course, you do. This bridge is very old and has seen more life in and around it than we could ever hope to live. Life isn't something that can be contained. We're all just vessels, containers if you will, that can only hold on to life for but a fleeting moment in all of eternity. Objects like this structure can hold on much longer. Life slowly leaks out of everything but living creatures like you and I lose it faster by giving our lives away to others. We lose it by loving, by sharing emotions, and by making connections with others. We lose our lives by slowly imprinting it on objects like this bridge. Do you understand?" he asked.

I nodded.

"If life can be imprinted in the beams that make this structure, it could certainly be found in the art we create. It can be imprinted in the clay used to sculpt, the paint used to paint, and in the photographs taken by artist such as yourself, would you agree? Here's what I believe. I believe the life in artistic objects are much stronger. They were molded and formed by the hands of a creator. Just as God created man and shared his electric charge of life with us, an artist shares his or her electric charge of life with his or her masterpiece."

Dorian threw his hands out wide.

"Imagine the power one could possess if you could harness that power for yourself!" he yelled.

During his rousing speech, I had been peeking at the surroundings through my camera and seeing the life, or 'electric charge of life' as he put it, all around me. When he spread his arms wide, I aimed my camera at him. Instead of a handsome young man, I again saw the glowing shadowy figure in his place. I snapped a picture.

"Sibyl, I'm telling you all of this because I can see you're special. You can see what I am saying is true. Please. Tell me you understand," he said. He grabbed me by my upper arms and pulled me close.

"You must see it. Don't you?" he asked.

His sudden change to apparent madness coupled with the dark image of him I saw through my camera frightened me. I didn't know what to say, so I played along.

"I think so," I said, nodding. "Yeah, I can see what you mean."

He gently held my face in his hands and kissed me on the forehead.

"My dear girl, I can see you have your doubts. Let me show you something that will make you truly believe."

We left the bridge and made our way to a gallery about two blocks away. Dorian pulled me along as we dodged patrons on the streets. He was mad with giddiness and muttered to himself all the way there.

We reached the gallery and entered through a side door.

"How do you have a key?" I asked.

"They're showing my art."

He rushed me through the exhibit so quickly, I didn't have time to see what was on display. But when he stopped at a locked door in the back of the exhibit, I had time to briefly look around. There were paintings all around that looked very old. No photos were on exhibit that I could see. A placard next to a painting of a Victorian-era woman seated under a tree read "All is Vanity - on loan from the Dorian Gray estate."

Dorian unlocked the door and pulled me into the back room.

"Are you Dorian Gray?" I asked.

He shut the door behind us without answering.

At that point, I began to worry. I'd seen enough crime shows to know when someone was about to be raped or murdered. I was no fool, but before I could make an attempt to escape, he uncovered the sole painting that had been resting against the wall.

The painting was revealed to be a portrait of a hideously grotesque man, a man that was vaguely familiar.

"This was the most beautiful portrait of me I'd ever seen, and it had so much life and beauty to give. Sadly, its well of life and healing is nearly dried up."

"This is a portrait of you?" I asked. "But…"

"It's hideous isn't it?" he asked. "Do you want to know why it is so hideous?"

Dorian pulled a knife out of his pocket and unsheathed it.

My initial thought was to run. I was sure he intended to kill me, but what he did next surprised me. He held out the blade for me to take.

"I want you to cut my face," he said.

"What?" I thought I must have misheard him. "You want me to cut you?"

"Yes, because only then will you finally understand," he said as he put the knife in my hand.

"You're crazy!" I shouted, as I turned to flee.

He grabbed my left arm and I instinctively swung at him with my right, slashing his face with the knife it held. The wound gushed blood down the side of his face. He grabbed my knife wielding hand and forced me to look at his wound.

He sneered as his face began to heal as if by magic. He nodded to the hideous painting, and to my astonishment, the gash appeared on the face in the painting.

"What the hell? How did you…?" I asked.

"It's not just a theory, Sibyl. You really can see life radiating from objects and people. Basil, the painter behind this portrait, could see it too. When I saw what he made, I struck a deal. The life in this portrait will continue to sustain me. I receive the life and beauty from the portrait until its well of life runs dry. That's why I need you. I need you to use your skills to take a photo of me. I need you to replace my painting with a photograph."

"Why me? Why a picture?" I asked.

"Why? Because a picture lasts forever my dear," he said with a chuckle.

"I need you because you can see what others can't. You can see the beauty and life that shines from your subject matter."

"What if I refuse?" I asked.

"Sibyl, my dear, I don't think you'll have much of a choice."

I struggled to break from his grip. I kicked him repeatedly, but he seemed to be impervious to my assault. He apparently couldn't be injured.

It was then that it hit me. The portrait. He said he needed to replace the portrait with a picture. He was implying that the portrait's well-being could impact him!

I kicked to the side, hitting the painting.

It had the effect I was looking for. As my foot went through the center of the painting, Dorian released my arm and doubled over in pain.

With my hands free from his grip, I was able to use the knife to slash the portrait to shreds. The face in the portrait began to look more like Dorian while Dorian became hideously deformed. He screamed with each slash of the canvas until the portrait was no longer recognizable and Dorian lied motionless in a pool of his own blood.

The authorities never found any evidence of his existence. The gallery of his paintings was empty. No shredded portrait or body was ever found. Of all the people in the park that night, no witnesses ever came forward to say they saw me with Dorian. I can't explain it. Could I have been imagining the whole thing? Could I have been losing my hold on reality? I don't think so. I've scoured over my photos and the last two photos on my camera from that day were of the yellow leaves at Lacks Park and a dark, under exposed shot of the underside of the Blue Bridge.

The photo from Lacks Park is the closest thing I could find to having evidence of meeting the elusive Dorian Gray. I've tried to brighten the image, but all I get is a dark shadow of a figure with outstretched arms. The face is grotesque and unrecognizable.

I no longer try to capture the glow I see in some of my photos. I've abandoned the artistic flare that led me to GVSU. I'm content taking pictures of the mundane and uninteresting. When I spy something utterly beautiful, or if I catch a glimpse of the glow emanating from a person or thing I'm trying to photograph, I put the camera down and enjoy the moment instead. I wouldn't want to capture or take someone or something's life light unintentionally.

It's best to let beauty be experienced rather than be captured. No person should be allowed to harness that beauty. I've seen the hideous results.

That Won't Hold Up in Court

by Jen Haeger

Candles flickered at equidistant points around the salt circle. Seated in the center, chanting under her breath, Hilary focused on the smear of blood soaked into the hardwood floorboards. She'd never summoned a recently departed spirit before, but she knew the basics. Find the thread of the spirit still left in the blood, draw it in by the energy of the sacred candles, and hold it with the crystal from the Peruvian ghost cave. Not really all that complicated as long as she didn't break the circle or mispronounce any of the Sanskrit derived incantations.

"That's not admissible in court."

The tension which had been building inside the circle dispersed in a rush of frigid air. She sighed and turned toward Glen Arbor's chief of police. "Lawrence, I've been sitting here for an hour and a half. Do you know how much sacred candles cost?"

Leaning against the door, the aging official's gut protruded over his belt, but still he managed to look dignified. "Do you really think you should be messing with the unseen powers on this one?"

"Why wouldn't I use all the resources at my disposal to solve a murder?"

He pushed off the doorframe and shrugged. "Thought Gladwin sent about a thousand evidence bags to the Staties." He offered her a hand.

She let him help her up. "He did."

"So, you don't trust them then?"

"No, I trust them." She dusted stray salt grains off her hands. "I just don't want to put all my eggs in one basket."

He pointed to the circle. "So, what were you doing anyway?"

Bending to blow out the wavering candles, she hesitated a beat. "Ah, you know, just one of my tracking-type spells."

One of his eyebrows tried to find his receding hairline. "Really?" He sighed. "You know I've always looked the other way with regards to your…unconventional methods, but this is a murder, Detective, not some bullshit petty theft case."

"Which is why I'm not just sitting around, crossing my fingers, and waiting for the lab to get back to us. I want to make sure we don't waste any time, Chief. There's a murderer on our streets. Are you able to sleep? 'Cuz I'm not."

He glanced down at the circle, then back up at her. "Fine. Do what you think you have to, but don't let it interfere with the real police work. We need evidence to convict this guy, not a trail of mystical energy." Turning away, he adjusted his hat. "And for all that's holy, don't let Gladwin see you messing up his crime scene."

Hilary let the chief leave without reminding him that Gladwin, having personally accompanied the forensic samples so as to make the chain of custody one link stronger, was still in Grayling. Staring down at the remnants of her interrupted ritual, she contemplated starting again, but quickly gave it up as a lost cause. The candles had spent their energies and the salt's purity waned by the minute. She'd have to start from scratch tomorrow night.

"Dammit Larry." She loved the chief, but he had no concept of the intricacies of the craft.

Having collected the half-melted candles, vacuumed up her salt circle, and resealed the crime scene, Hilary was back in her own little bungalow with the case file, a beer, and a white board recently purchased from the Staples in Traverse City. The beer dripped condensation onto her white, wicker coffee table as she stared at the board. There wasn't much to it.

A timeline of events, as best they could glean, ran along the bottom of the board: from when the last patron had left Higgin's Bar to the time of death. The last person to see Chelsea Davis alive and the first suspect was Ed Paconni, a local, a regular, and a drunk. But he was alibied by his wife, having stumbled in and passed out in the living room well before Chelsea's time of death. Mrs. Paconni could've been lying of course, but Gladwin cleared the Paconni household based on lack of evidence and Ed having the wrong shoe size and type.

The next suspect was Chelsea's ex-boyfriend, Hue Yong, but he was verified as having been in Ann Arbor attending a biomedical engineering grad school reception until well after midnight the night of the murder. He would've had to break every speed limit on the way to reach Glen Arbor to kill Chelsea around 3a.m., clean up, then break them all again to get back and be seen in his research lab at 7a.m. the next morning. Not impossible, but very unlikely considering the Staties loved to lurk on the expressways heading north in the summer, and there were no condemning tickets or traffic stops. Also, there was a lack of motive there. The break-up, by all accounts, had been amiable.

Then there was…nope, that was it. Two suspects. No one remembered anyone bothering Chelsea Friday night or her refusing to serve anyone. It'd been a typical summer night of half townies and half tourists celebrating the coming weekend at Higgin's, but everyone seemed to have gotten along.

Hilary tore her gaze away from the board and snatched up her warming bottle of Edmund Fitzgerald. "Damn. Had to be some tourist looking for an Up North tryst." She took a long swig. "Someone nice enough, but not overly friendly." She burped and set the beer down again. They'd tried to track down all the tourists who'd patronized the bar the night of the murder, but only a few had used their credit cards, and of those, no one stood out. The phone rang. Shaking her head, she traipsed into the kitchen to answer and grab a bag of pretzels.

"Hello."

"Detective Parekh, this is Dr. Lambert. I was just wondering how the case was coming along."

Hilary rolled her eyes. With Dr. Ryma, the town's general medical practitioner, on an extended vacation to Hawaii, coroner duties had fallen between Dr. Lambert, the local veterinarian, and Dr. Hernandez, the dentist. Hilary now wished she'd chosen the dentist. "Sorry Dr. Lambert, like I told you, I can't really discuss details of an open case."

"Not even with the official coroner?"

"Nope. Sorry." Hilary wanted to bang her head against the phone.

"Well, you let me know if you need anything else from me. Chelsea was a lovely girl and I want to help in any way that I can."

"I know you do, Dr. Lambert. I promise I'll let you know if there's anything you can do."

"Oh, alright." Dr. Lambert cleared her throat. "Also, I wanted to let you know that Pongo is due for his vaccines August first."

"Thank you, Dr. Lambert. Goodbye now."

"Goodnight."

After she put the phone down, Hilary chewed on her bottom lip. Dr. Lambert's nosiness would make her suspicious if she wasn't normally a bit flakey and scatterbrained. Pretzels in hand, Hilary returned to the living room, picked up a dry-erase marker, and took off the cap. Hand poised over the white board, she peered down at her sleeping pug, grimaced, and recapped it.

"Nah."

Hilary's second attempt at the ritual the next night was successful. More or less. The spirit of Chelsea Davis materialized inside the salt circle over the blood stain much like ice crystals encapsulating a blade of grass in a high-speed time lapse. Not that the ghost had weird, prickly sharp edges. She was a smooth shade and not a mimeograph of Chelsea's beaten and bloody remains, but an image of the young woman in perfect health and vitality sheathed in a translucent white robe. Well, the whole figure was white, not just the robe. More of a chalked impression of Chelsea than a photograph.

The thrill of success faded quickly, however, when Hilary realized that the spirit couldn't hear Hilary or make any noise. In retrospect, she should've anticipated this complication, but undeterred she took up a pen and pad of paper.

Her first communication attempt: YOU ARE DEAD, with a hastily added: I'M SORRY.

The ghost frowned, looked around the disheveled apartment, down at the blood stain on the floor, back up at Hilary, and then nodded.

DO YOU KNOW WHO KILLED YOU?

The ghost's frown deepened, delicate eyebrows knitting in concentration, eyes taking on a faraway quality, before she held up a sculpted hand with the flat of the palm facing down and tilted it from side to side.

Uncomprehending, Hilary blinked. Clearly it was a yes or no question and she was about to ask it a different way when the answer struck her: sort of. Okay.

DO YOU KNOW YOUR KILLER'S NAME?

The ghost perked up and shook her head.

Now they were getting somewhere.

MALE?

Nod.

BLOND?

Shake.

BROWN HAIR?

Nod.

Fantastic.

Three hours later Hilary was having trouble coming up with questions and the ghost, though she still stood very straight and poised, wore a lackluster expression. It was now clear the murderer was a tourist who'd come into Higgin's bar a few nights before the murder and paid cash. Chelsea didn't remember a name or if he said where he was staying or for how long. He hadn't hit on her that night, and she was shocked to find him in her apartment wielding her kitchen knife when she came home early Saturday morning. This information coupled with a vague description wasn't much to go on, but at least Hilary could stop harassing locals and people who were at the bar on Friday night.

She glanced up from her notes into the spirit's dulled eyes.

ARE YOU TIRED?

Chelsea shook her head.

Hilary narrowed her eyes.

BORED?

The ghost made the "sort of" gesture again.

Hilary chortled and Chelsea smiled, but then Hilary realized she hadn't really been thinking about the spirit and what this all meant or felt like to her. It wasn't really Chelsea standing in front of her, but still. I'm such an ass.

YOU OKAY WITH THIS?

The shade's brows furrowed and she cocked her head.

BEING HERE. HELPING ME.

Chelsea's face brightened and she nodded.

Other questions formed in Hilary's mind. Where the ghost had come from for starters. Was there an afterlife or was she more like a residual memory? Existential secrets of the universe questions. But now wasn't the time. Hilary had been hoping for a name, but the spirit could still be useful. It was possible the killer would stick around town to watch the aftermath of his crime. He might even go back to Higgin's for a celebratory drink.

WILL YOU COME WITH ME?

Face darkening, the spirit pointed down at the salt circle.

"Ah, right."

I'LL MAKE AN OPENING.

Hilary pointed to the large, black crystal in a silver bowl at the most northern edge of the circle.

CRYSTAL SHOULD ACT AS ANCHOR.

The spirit hesitated briefly then nodded.

Hilary put down the pen and paper pad, got down on her hands and knees, and swept a narrow opening in the ring of salt. She could've just smudged the circle's integrity with her foot, but it seemed crude in front of Chelsea. Standing, she watched the ghost. The first good news, it was still there. If Hilary hadn't done everything right or the crystal was flawed, breaking the circle would've dispelled the gathered energies holding Chelsea's spirit together. So far so good.

The spirit didn't move at first and Hilary gave her an encouraging smile as she palmed the crystal. Forehead wrinkling and lips pressed tight, it took one tentative step toward the opening, then another, then eased a bare, spectral foot outside the circle and then snatched it back and appraised it, toes wiggling. Convinced the foot was undamaged, Chelsea plunged through the opening like a dry child jumping into Lake Superior. When she stood, in one piece, on the outside of the circle, Hilary let out a breath she didn't realize she'd been holding. Magic was tricky and any number of unpleasant things could happen if you got it wrong. Particularly when doing things like raising spirits of the dead. She smiled at the ghost.

"Good. Alright. Let's go."

It was only mostly bizarre walking around town with the shade of a dead woman which only you could see in tow. The trick was the crystal. In order for someone to observe the spirit outside the salt circle, they had to be touching the ghost crystal…or have an innate ability to perceive spirits, which was pretty rare. Even so, it was hard to believe the translucent white, glowing remnant of the former waitress was completely invisible as Hilary entered Higgin's and all heads turned toward her. And a lot of heads there were. The bloody crime was the only murder in Glen Arbor anyone remembered and morbid fascination drew them into the bar like flies onto a corpse.

Nodding to a few of the regulars and trying not to look at Chelsea, Hilary made her way towards the bar. Cathy, Higgin's other waitress, was filling her tray with drinks, a harrowed expression marring her painted-on good looks. She spotted Hilary and nudged a patron at the bar, Tommy, the assistant manager of the local hardware store and coincidentally the owner's son.

"Hey, Tommy, you got two strong legs, let the Detective take a load off."

Tommy looked up from contemplating the dregs of his beer, a gap-toothed smile splitting his face as he recognized Hilary which was fast replaced by a mask of remembered concern. He scrambled off the barstool into half of Chelsea. "Hey Hilary, how's the case coming?"

Choking on a swallow at the ghost's indignity, Hilary coughed out a reply as she sat. "Oh, it's coming. Can't talk about it really."

The bartender, Marty, his attention drawn by the coughing fit, hurried over with a glass of water. "I assume you'll want something stronger in a minute."

Hilary sipped the water and cleared her throat. Chelsea's spirit had shifted into the bar so no one would walk through her again, still Marty's hand penetrated her chest as he bussed an empty glass.

"Yeah, can I get an Oberon?"

He grinned and winked. "You got it."

She didn't bother to specify a size. No matter what she said, he'd bring a twenty ounce. Her gaze drifted to the spirit's wandering eyes scanning the bar's interior.

"Taking a break?"

"Huh? Oh, yeah, Tommy. Just needed to get out of my house for a while." She attempted an I-know-we-used-to-date-but-I-really-don't-want-to-chat-right-now glare, but Tommy didn't notice.

"Gladwin still in Grayling?"

"Yep. Someone has to oversee the evidence analysis."

Marty returned with her oversized glass of beer and she gulped it dutifully.

"How long has he been there? Geez, I think that guy thinks he's Grissom from CSI or something."

"Uh huh." Hilary pretended to watch Sports Center on the television above the bar while she continued to scrutinize the spirit's face.

"You know, Chelsea and I dated once."

Hilary narrowly avoided a spit take. "You did?"

Tommy bobbed his head. "In middle school. I asked her to a school dance, but at the end of the night she made me promise that we were just friends." He laughed, but then stopped himself in a stifled hiccup and stared at the floor. "She was really nice."

Caught between not wanting to encourage Tommy and wanting to do her job, Hilary took another swig of beer and glanced sidelong at Chelsea to make sure her expression hadn't changed. It hadn't.

"So, Tommy, were you here at Higgin's the Wednesday before?"

He looked up, his eyes red and moist. "Before what?"

She stared at him blankly.

"Oh, before the...before Chelsea...Um, no, no I was working late Wednesday. Why?"

"Just following up on a lead."

His face fell a bit more. "Oh. Sorry I can't help."

Hilary offered him a small smile then peeked over at Chelsea again. The ghost saw her, frowned and shook its head.

"Me too."

For the next two days Hilary walked around Glen Arbor hunting for Chelsea's murderer. During the day she almost couldn't see her spectral shadow trailing by her side and would have to retreat to the shadows of a tree or alleyway to make sure the spirit hadn't spotted her killer and was trying to get Hilary's attention. But her face always wore the same mournful disappointment. It seemed the killer tourist hadn't stuck around town after all. He was probably getting enough of a buzz off the media swarm whose mosquito-like reporters were getting harder and harder to avoid.

A sullen Gladwin came back from Grayling with the killer's DNA profile, a partial thumbprint, a size ten Nike Air Max 95 shoe print, and trace fiber evidence, but neither the offender's fingerprints nor genetic profile were in the system and with no viable suspects, there was nothing to compare the evidence to.

"I say we run DNA from everyone in town!" Gladwin slammed his fist down on Hilary's desk.

"Gladwin, even if we had the funds for that, do you really think the killer's going to give consent? I already let you run Hue and Ed's DNA even though we'd ruled them out. We need a real suspect."

Hilary peered over his shoulder at Chelsea. The spirit had taken on a haggard appearance and her outline showed fraying around the edges. Again, it wasn't surprising. Energies always dissipated, especially those unnaturally coalesced like those holding Chelsea together. But it meant Hilary was running out of time with her only lead.

She'd hoped that the DNA or fingerprints would lead to a suspect and then the ghost could confirm, no such luck. She could've attempted a tracking spell like she'd done a bunch of times with other minor crimes in the area, but she needed something belonging to the killer. Unfortunately, Gladwin, double-certified in crime-scene evidence collection, had scoured Chelsea's apartment for two days and guarded his evidence bags like a Doberman before sending it all to the Staties. In the absence of a miracle eye witness or anonymous tip, it looked like Chelsea's murderer was going to get away with it.

Hilary's guts twisted in her stomach. She wanted to throw up. She'd been so sure that between Gladwin's evidence and Chelsea's spirit, they'd be able to get the guy. Now she had to tell the ravaged ghost her murder would probably never be solved, that her killer would never see justice. This was exactly the type of big-city horror Hilary had left Chicago to get away from.

That night in her little house, the eyes of a murdered woman following her every move, Hilary drank, Journeyman's Last Feather Rye whiskey this time, and contemplated her options. She could drive down to Grayling and try to get the Staties to give her back some of the precious evidence even though she could give them no good reason to do so. She could get online, become a quick study in suspect sketching and try to draw a likeness of the killer off interpretations of the mute victim's facial expressions and gestures. Not likely a profitable endeavor with her artistic skills. She could drag Chelsea's ghost around to some neighboring towns and try to get lucky before the spirit faded away completely. Or…

THERE'S ONE MORE THING WE CAN DO.

The phone's shrill tone cut right through Hilary's whiskey-soaked hangover like a chainsaw. Pawing at it blindly as the noise split open her skull, she finally swiped answer and brought the cell to her ear. "Detective Parekh."

The chief's voice was strained. "Put on some pants. There's been another murder."

The Up North Motel was technically outside of town, but still had a Glen Arbor address. The manager, responding to a complaint of screaming coming from room 4, had opened it to find a man stabbed to death with his own hunting knife. No sign of forced entry, though a bathroom window was ajar.

Hilary and the chief had entered the room, but hadn't touched the body. They hadn't bothered with paramedics. The man was obviously dead, and they were waiting for Dr. Lambert, damn you Dr. Ryma, to get there to release the body. Brown hair, Nike Air Max 95 shoes, and Hilary was sure the DNA and thumbprint would be a match; case closed. Fueled by gruesome crime scene photos, with her last bit of residual energy and a little boost from Hilary's spell, Chelsea's unleashed spirit had found him. Justice had been served, more or less. The chief, more observant than most gave his slovenly appearance credit for, gave her a hard look.

"I'm not going to find any evidence here that I'm not going to like, am I?"

Hilary fingered the crystal shards in her pocket, the whisper of a smile sneaking onto her face. "No sir. At least nothing that'll hold up in court."

No Country for Old Blobs

by Matthew Tansek

The storm door slammed behind Joline Cray as she charged out of her house shotgun in hand. She had lost too many of her animals to coyotes in the past month and she was going to make damn sure she didn't lose another. But as the door banged shut behind her mind spun with the image in front of her; had her farm been somehow been thrown into space? She wiped her eyes, willing them to adjust to the darkness faster, and felt panic as she heard the ululations of one of her goats in distress. What stretched out before her was the flat fields of her property, but it was as if the whole of them were covered in a glistening mirror, so that the clear night sky above reflected off of the shimmering ground and hid any sense of the horizon amidst the sea of twinkling starlight.

Joline took a tentative step off of the porch, holding onto the railing for safety, and found that her slipper only sunk into the substance a half inch or so. She stepped off with her other foot and immediately found that whatever it was stuck to her feet like tar. Was it oil? Did this have something to do with that new fracking operation that had sprung up not far down the road? The suction noises of her feet punctuated the night air as she made her way to the barn. As she got close however she could see that there was a feature of the terrain that was different, a hill where a hill had not been before. She wished she had grabbed her phone instead of her gun when she had charged outside. She moved a few more steps towards it and saw in the feeble light that something translucent, as if a great heap of the substance that lay tacky over the ground was collected there. She could make out several things adrift within, a potted plant that had sat in the front yard, paving stones from the walkway, and then the fur and features of one of the goats, its dead eyes staring wide.

A reactive step back that did not release from the ground sent Joline off balance and falling. Where her elbows hit the substance she was immediately aware of a stinging sensation and then a rippling effect that seemed to radiate outward in all directions. She scrambled to her feet watching as the ripple sent the whole of the massive hill of the stuff quivering. She ran for the door of her house as the hill rolled towards her. She turned, running wild. She fired a blast from her shotgun into the substance which splattered against its surface like a stone tossed into a still pond. As she reached the porch she could feel the whole of her feet sinking into the stuff which became deeper as the mass of it grew closer to her. It felt as if her feet were on fire as her slippers were lost and her bare skin up to her ankles was submerged. With a scream, her right hand flung forward to the handle of the door. She felt her body plunge up to her knees as a suction within the goo pulled her up off of the ground. The pain was almost overwhelming as her skin reacted to the corrosive fluid, but her adrenaline won the contest. She could feel herself pulling free and forward. She had almost made it through and to the door when a great black-green gob plopped onto the wood of the porch next to her. Joline pulled her blistering flesh free and twisted her head to look up in time to see a great mass of the substance rolling over the edge of her roof to cascade slowly down upon her.

Moxy Bauhoff stood at the edge of the wastewater pit in the shadow of the well tower and gazed into its depths. There was something moving down there, shifting with the sand, a slightly darker color than the rest of the stuff down there. As she watched, a glistening green bubble came floating slowly to the surface of the water and scooted like a limbless turtle towards the edge once it had reached the surface.

"Buck get over here and take a look at this thing," she shouted, crouching down and pulling out her cell phone to take a picture of it, "quick Buck, come here!"

Buck, always slow to react, downed the rest of his Coke and chucked the can into a bin next to the propped exterior door of the site trailer, and made his way over. "Please don't tell me there is something going wrong," he said as he walked up, "my daughter's birthday's this week and my emotions just can't take it if I have to miss it because of unexpected delays."

"What is this thing?" Moxy said, luring the greenish bubble around in a circle with her finger.

"Shit, that's weird. Is it a jellyfish?" Buck said, crouching down and shading his eyes from the beating sun, "the only stuff that should be in there is flow-back from the injection. Whatever it is it must have come in from out here. I don't know what sort of stuff they have out here in the boonies of Michigan, but that's a new one to me."

Moxy continued to lure it back and forth as it chased after her outstretched finger watching as it trailed a clear slime behind it as it went along, "Well keep an eye on it for a second, will you? I'm going to find a jar or something to put it in."

"For real? You want to keep the ball of snot?"

Moxy smiled broadly, "What? It clearly likes me. Where's your scientific sense of curiosity?"

"We're chemists not biologists, and besides even if we are the first humans to discover North America's elusive snot goblin, you really want that named after you?"

"Just help me out, this sort of thing is the only real perk of doing this job."

"What sort of thing?"

"You know, the time-wasting kind where you find a distraction in a new place."

Buck sighed, "I hear you, collecting site data from these remote fracking sites isn't the most exciting thing in the world."

Ten minutes later Moxy and Buck were back inside sitting at the only table inside marveling at the strange thing in the pickle jar between them.

"When Jacob comes to give Rebecca Herve a tour, are you going to add this to the list of attractions?" Buck asked, cleaning his glasses on his shirt.

"I would have if I didn't think putting it in the jar somehow killed it," she tapped the side of the glass and watched as the green blob within it floated motionlessly, "It looks like there was some kind of connective tissue that I must have accidentally hurt. Poor little guy,"

"What a shame," Buck said in an emotionless tone, "go and dump it outside and pull up the sensor reports so we can have that stuff ready for when they get here."

"You do want to get out of here on time don't you?"

"These are supposed to be remote fracking operations. Us being here kinda defeats that premise doesn't it?"

"I think you're just nervous. It was your new cocktail that got greenlit Buck, take some credit for the ingenuity, you managed to find a way to pillage a little bit more out of Mother Earth."

"I didn't just find the right amount of ingredients, I found the formula for determining the right amount of ingredients. Every place is different you know, one shale is not quite the same as the next shale, so you need a way to analyze it and adjust the acids, stabilizers, friction reducers, etc."

Moxy grabbed the jar and headed back outside to dump her short-lived discovery.

Jacob Pettin was a curly-haired, pale, brown-noser and Moxy and Buck's direct supervisor. Due to the remote nature of their work, they rarely interacted face to face, and to see them next to one another in the flesh was almost a comedy of differences. The occasion that brought them together on this sunny afternoon was the new Automated Fracking Appliance version 3.0, and the first field test of Buck's new formula of injection chemicals. Rebecca Herve was a sometimes C suite executive sometimes politician who was more than a little financially motivated to see these new operations in action.

"So you can see that with the new articulated set of sensors mounted right to the drilling platform our system can, in real-time, make adjustments to what's going on down there in the fracking zone," Jacob continued as he and the portly woman walked through the installation, "our trailer here is just for these initial testing phases for our research team to make sure this launch is meeting our performance expectations; and spoiler alert, they are."

Buck thought that if there was a drinking game for every time he had heard Jacob say spoiler alert, he would be face down dead of alcohol poisoning already.

"You have no idea how happy this makes me, to be actually able to utilize this dormant land without the tremendous overhead of extraction the old-fashioned way," Rebecca said, "whole new vistas are going to open up for what we can offer here."

"I mean, leaving places open to nature is still a valid way of utilizing them right? Not every inch of space needs to be hyper profitable."

Rebecca gave an audible snort at this, "I understand that this is totally safe, isn't that right? It's not like nature and profits are mutually exclusive."

Jacob shot Moxy daggers, "That's right Ms. Herve, the bears with their honey can sleep safely without so much as an inkling about what is going on over here. They, spoiler alert, don't care what is going on hundreds of feet below the earth."

Moxy shook her head thinking, did Jacob's whole idea about bears come from Winni the Pooh?

The tour continued for another ten minutes or so before they heard the crunch of tire treads on the gravel. Moxy caught a glimpse of the black and white of a police cruiser through the trees.

The four of them exchanged looks as the police cruiser parked next to Jacob's rented town car.

"Afternoon folks," the officer said as he got out of his car and straightened his police-issued cap, "I'm Officer Heartwell, I was hoping I might have a word with you all if you have a moment."

"Of course, officer," said Jacob obsequiously, "I'm Jacob Pettin, and this is Ms. Herve one of the masterminds behind this operation."

The officer nodded and looked to Buck and Moxy.

"Oh yes, and these are some of the technical staff that assist in the operation," Jacob added, "is there a problem officer?"

"I can assure you that we have all of the necessary permissions and went through proper channels to be here," said Rebecca through a smiling facade.

"I'm sure you did, no. There was an incident at a nearby farm not too far from here. More than anything I just came out here just to make sure that you all were all right."

"What happened?" Buck asked.

"We're still working that out, it looks like there might have been some exposure to some dangerous chemicals."

"Fracking gets a bad rap in the press officer, but I promise you that there is nothing that we are doing that could have possibly exposed anyone to anything harmful," Jacob said gesturing to the machinery. "Our procedure only affects levels far below the water table, perfectly safe and out of range of anything that anyone would ever notice. We were just discussing its minimal effects on nature just a moment ago."

"Hey now, I'm not pointing any fingers," the officer said, "like I said I just wanted to make sure that everything was OK over here and that you haven't seen anything out of the ordinary."

"What kind of chemical exposure?" Maxine asked stepping forward and offering her hand, "I'm Maxine Bauhauff and this is Dorius Buckly, we're chemists for the Argos Energy Group. If you can't tell us anything I understand, I've seen a few cop shows on TV."

The officer nodded, "I couldn't tell you, I've never seen anything like it. We have procedures in place for incidents of suspected disease or outbreaks or what have you. But I could really use a second opinion. If you wouldn't mind coming with me to take a look, it might give us a jump on dealing with whatever caused this."

"I'm sorry but we are in the middle of an assessment of the installation and our schedules couldn't accommodate--" Jacob began but then was cut off by Moxy.

"Buck can stay here and show you the process and how the levels of his new injection compound are working out. I'll go take a look at whatever might have gone on."

Jacob's infant-like face showed his disgust.

"It would be good if we showed that we care about what happens around here," Moxy offered, forgetting just how big of a little dictator her boss could be, especially in front of someone he was trying to impress.

"She has a point," Rebecca said, "why don't you go with her and make sure that we do all that we can."

"Me? I don't know if that's really necessary," Jacob said.

"Nonsense, I'm sure you will be back within an hour," Rebecca said eyeing Buck predatorily, "besides it will give me a chance to get to know some of the staff here a little better."

Buck locked eyes with Moxy and shook his head in distress.

Jacob had a few choice things to say to Moxy as they rode in the back of the police car to the nearby farm. It would have bothered her if she wasn't wrapped up in the curiosity about what might have happened. Did farmers these days use some chemicals to treat their fields that she didn't know about? Was about the only thing she could think of that might be responsible for a woman losing her life.

They pulled up fifty feet outside of a pleasant-looking white house about a quarter mile off of the main road. Scenic rural views of the fields that surrounded the house made it a picturesque scene.

As soon as Moxy set a foot down on the soil she could tell something was off about the scene. There was a crunch to the ground that was far from normal. The smell of mildew hung in the air. The house also seemed off, glossy in a weird way, like the siding was covered in saran wrap.

"You can see this struck us as peculiar. As soon as we arrived on the scene we could see this stuff covering everything." Officer Heartwell said, looking across the large yard that spanned the front of the house.

"Is it poisonous?" Jacob asked.

"No, nothing about it is harmful. Our limited testing determined it to be hygroscopic, meaning it absorbs moisture from the environment and is 96 percent water. It also contains proteins, sugar, and salt."

"That's peculiar. Sounds like mucus or snail slime." Moxy said scraping some up from the ground and looking at it more closely.

Jacob gave a disgusted face and looked regrettably at his expensive Italian shoes.

"Peculiar is one word for it, considering what was found at the rear of the house. One of the farm hands spotted it when they came in. Stay here on this path and I'll walk you over," Heartwell paused, "You understand that anything that you see here is to be kept to yourselves for the time being?"

Jacob and Moxy agreed, and the three of them rounded the rear of the house. There were several other figures wearing specialized badges working around the area. On the center of the front porch were unmistakably human remains. Jacob covered his mouth and stopped dead in his tracks as Moxy craned her neck for a better view.

"Joline Cray, 41, you can see what we have determined to be acid burns to the entirety of the remains."

"She got splashed with acid?" Jacob asked through his hand.

"Not splashed, submerged is more like it. Every inch of her remains shows signs of exposure to a highly corrosive substance." Heartwell said, "Considering the state of this place our theories are a little strained. Any ideas Ms. Bauhoff?"

"I honestly don't know if I'm going to be all that helpful. It seems like anything I might have thought you already have a handle on," Moxy said, her mind trying to spin a theory that could account for the strangeness that she was looking at, "There doesn't seem to be much left of her, do you think that she was dumped here?"

"Not sure what I think just yet, like as I said. But the loaded shotgun there beside the victim with her prints on the handle makes me think that she was trying to defend herself from…" Heartwell waved his hand in an unknowing kind of way.

Jacob ushered Moxy back away from the porch, "Well officer, I'm sorry that we couldn't be more helpful, but it looks like you have things well in hand. This falls well outside our business I'm afraid."

The absolute lack of curiosity that ran through her coworkers frustrated Moxy, but Jacob was right there didn't seem to be any insight that she could offer.

After another minute of silent conjecture, the three began their walk back to the car.

"Perhaps something was dropped from a plane, spreading this stuff everywhere and the woman out back just was caught up in it," Jacob said.

The sun, now reaching its zenith cast a bright light down on the flat farmlands of Michigan's interior, and as she looked at it Moxy saw a distant glistening near the horizon that looked remarkably like the effect the light was having on the dried translucent substance that they had just passed through.

"Do you see that?" she asked, pointing East.

It was indeed another location with the same substance smeared across it, and before too long they had traveled to two other locations, each showing signs of being covered in the same translucent fluid as the farm. Each time they spotted the next location hundreds of feet away. Moxy hated to think that Jacob was onto something, but perhaps he was right. What else could explain the distance between each site if it had not been dropped from the sky?

"Jesus, I see the next one," Heartwell said having only stepped from the driver's seat only for a moment. Moxy saw it too. They had been traveling more or less in a straight line, and that line had led them directly to the edge of the small town of Fife Lake.

"We would have heard about it if people got hurt, so this last spot here must be the end of it, right?" Jacob asked, his voice sounding like it was trying to convince himself just as much as it was us.

"We haven't received any calls about anything," Heartwell said diving back into the car, "not yet anyway."

Heartwell drove his cruiser like a madman, blasting the siren as he came to the edge of the town. The first building off of the interstate was a gas station and sandwich shop combo. Moxy and Jacob held on for dear life as the car whipped around and came to a screeching halt.

"You two wait here, I'm going to warn everybody of a possibly dangerous situation and get them to evacuate the area," Heartwell said stepping out of the still-running car.

Moxy fished her phone out from where it had fallen to the floor in the commotion and called Buck.

"Where have you been? I've been fighting off this woman's pervy advances for the past--"

"Listen, there is something happening. It just occurred to me, you know that bubble of green slime that we fished out of the wastewater?"

"Yeah," Buck said incredulously.

"Well, that was just like a baby one or something maybe. Holy fuck-" Moxy's jaw dropped as she watched the landscape behind the gas station suddenly change. It started out like a puddle had suddenly formed in the center of the scrubby gravel-strewn field, but as she watched the puddle grew until a mound, and then several mounds of semi-translucent green slime rose up over the ground and began rolling towards the building like waves of water.

"Are you fucking seeing this?" Jacob asked half climbing out of the car to see it more clearly, "what the fuck am I looking at?"

What the waves of slime lacked in speed as they moved they more than made up for in solid impact as they collided with the side of the building with the sandwich shop, smashing straight through the windows and spilling far into the building.

Screams could be heard, and through the glass entry doors to the building, Moxy could see Heartwell moving to help those that clearly had been hit by the deluge.

"Fuck this, we are so out of here," Jacob said exiting the back of the vehicle and making his way to the driver's seat.

"You can't just take off and leave the policeman," Moxy shouted.

"The fuck I can't," Jacob said becoming more panicky as they watched several more of the fifteen-foot-wide green domes rise up from the adjacent lot and begin their slow roll toward the gas station, hitting different points and enveloping nearly half of the perimeter of the structure.

Jacob slammed the accelerator, nearly hitting a woman and her two kids that were fleeing from the building, and pulled quickly out onto the road.

Moxy tried to shout a warning, but it was too late as tires screeched and a pickup truck, clearly driving distracted by the sight of what was happening slammed into the driver's side of the police cruiser. Moxy was aware of the crash of glass, the bang of inflating airbags, and her head slamming hard against the side of the door that was impacted before falling momentarily unconscious.

The taste of blood and the throbbing of her head roused Moxy some minutes later. She instinctively fished her phone, now with a badly cracked screen, from the floor of the car. She surveyed her surroundings. The slime had continued to spill up from the ground but rather than in large clumps, it pooled over the ground like flooding water. The gas station was covered in translucent residue, and if there was life still inside of it there was no sign. Several dark forms floated beneath the green surface. Moxy shivered, although she only half knew why.

"My fucking seatbelt won't release," Jacob said from the driver's seat, having clearly suffered worse from the impact than Moxy had. He struggled against the straps and the mangled door helplessly.

"One second, I'll come around and see if I can help you," Moxy said thickly as she slid to the passenger side and opened the door.

Outside of the door, however, she could see that the ground was covered in the green substance, slowly undulating outward from the point it had appeared. She watched mesmerized by the network of veins that ran through it. She wondered if it wasn't some sort of gigantic slime mold or relative of one, pulsing to locomote across the ground.

"Holy sweet mother of Christ!" Jacob said, his voice rising in panic as he saw the green slime beginning to push its way up the side of the police car and onto the hood in front of him. He railed against the straps, and Moxy could hear the ratcheting of the seatbelt gripping him tighter.

Stepping down into the goo was not a good option. Thanking herself for always wearing practical shoes she hoisted herself up onto the top of the car, stepping on the wreckage of the window to give herself the leverage to twist around and up.

"Hold on Jacob," she called out moving to the passenger side door and reaching down and opening it.

"Figures I hit a damn cop," the driver of the pickup said, following Moxy's lead and climbing up and into the open bed of the vehicle, "you alright?"

"Yeah, but my boss is trapped inside," she said turning to drop her head over the edge of the roof and look inside.

Inside the car, things had gotten considerably worse. The slime had made its way up through the inside of the car and was spewing out through the vents. When it hit Jacob's knees and thighs he could feel a stinging sensation that was steadily growing more severe. He tried to wipe it away with his hands, but upon contact with his skin, the stuff seemed to become more excited. It felt like his hands were being held to the top of a slowing heating stove burner. By the time Moxy had poked her head down from the top of the car the pain had become unbearable.

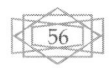

Jacob screamed and thrashed as more of the green substance poured over him, coating his legs and chest and working its way up, fanning out against his skin, defying gravity. His body convulsed, and he threw his head back and forth, clawing at his mouth with slime-covered hands in an attempt to keep it away from his face. This only made things worse. Through the translucent green tint of the layer of slime, Moxy could see Jacob's skin reddening and dissolving. Windows through his epidermis opened to reveal the quivering sinews beneath. When it had reached his nose and eyes his screams became violent vomiting bursts. She pulled her head back around to avoid being struck with the splatter of his final moments.

Dazed and horrified, Moxy looked across to the man standing in the back of the pickup. He was perhaps in his sixties with a full grey beard and a mesh hat. He shook his head solemnly and in disbelief. She somehow was glad to have not witnessed Jacob's death alone.

Although nothing was said between them for a long moment they both seemed to say the same thing on their faces. So what the hell are we supposed to do now? They looked at the spreading substance, the fleeing people, and the cars stopping on the road.

Then just as quickly as it has spread out. the veins that ran through the substance began retracting. The pooling substance rolled back onto itself piling up and slurping its way back towards the lot behind the gas station.

"This ain't no chemical spill," the man in the hat said, clearly voicing out loud some line of internal argument he was having with himself.

Moxy was hesitant to touch the glistening surface where the slime had been. It was similar to the slime trail a slug leaves behind as it moved. This validated what she had been thinking. After all of the green material vanished from view she jumped off of the car. What remained of her boss made her sick to her stomach, so she stumbled forward to where the slime had come from, her desire for answers overpowering her sense of self-preservation.

Where the slime had come up from the ground there was a tremendous amount of clear residue, but otherwise, there was nothing to see. She had half expected to see some sort of tunnel or trail where the thing had come from, but there was nothing. It must have been traveling underground she thought.

There were sirens in the distance. Their noise shook her from her stupor. She pulled out her phone and called Buck again.

It occurred to her that the bubble of the green stuff that they had found matched exactly to what she had just seen in a much larger form. It made her think two things, the first was the possibility that what they were doing maybe was actually responsible, and the second thing was how she had so easily killed whatever it was by placing it in the pickle jar.

"You OK kid?" Buck asked.

"Nope, I'm really not OK Buck. I just watched some sort of slime dissolve our boss,"

"Say that again?"

"Jacob is dead Buck; I watched a huge version of that green thing we had in the jar earlier just dissolve him in front of my eyes."

There was silence on the phone as Buck tried to process what he just heard and decide what, if any of it, to take seriously.

As Moxy stood there her eyes drifted to the field of neglected land that lead behind the gas station down parallel to the street. There was, distinctly, a trail of glossy substance forming that seemed to sparkle in the sunlight.

"Oh Jesus Buck, I think the thing is still moving. I think it is going to attack the next building here in town. Maybe the whole town, if the thing is big enough. Fuck, this is going to get really bad."

"Calm down, are you with the officer that came and picked you up? Get him to drive you someplace safe. I'll grab my keys and pick you up."

"He's gone, I think he might be dead too, I don't know. I don't know anything."

"That thing you caught earlier, do you really think it was a baby version? Or a part of it or something?"

"It kinda looks like a slime mold in the way it moves or, you know, the way I think a giant slime mold would move it was as big as a god damn bus."

"So maybe fungicides would hurt it? Neem oil, sulfur, that sort of thing?"

"You know what I think? I think that maybe the fracking station was a part of its path, or maybe we opened up a path for it through the shale barrier."

"That's a leap. We only saw a small one here. Look, just get to someplace safe and call me back. I've got the keys and I'll start heading toward you."

Moxy looked at the next buildings down the line, a cute little antique shop, and garden center. "What would it take to set that next injection with a giant amount of biocide?"

"Since we brought a lot of the materials with us, I could set that up in a couple of minutes, but Moxy we aren't sure if whatever it is you are seeing came from here, or is even still here."

"All of the slime is interconnected, there are like veins that run through it like what you would see in a plant leaf or something. If it came through the fracking station that's going to be where the trunk of the tree is, you follow me? Or at least further back up the plant than where I am here."

"That sounds like a long shot, but like what the hell, I'll set it up."

"Thanks, Buck. I gotta go."

Moxy hung up the phone and started running toward the garden center. Most of the people that were there had come out and were gawking at the chaos of the gas station, completely unaware that there was something moving right at their feet. That they were about to be consumed by a giant predatory slime monster.

Maybe some of the gawkers heard her screaming, maybe they saw her flailing her arms, but none of them, not a single one moved back. About 30 feet away Moxy saw that it was too late, the subtle glisten that she has seen in the sunlight had been replaced with a darker, stickier substance, and Moxy saw several of the onlookers pulling up their shoes and moving awkwardly as they became aware of being stuck to the ground.

Moxy almost didn't want to watch, visions of Jacob's last moments flashing intensely in her mind. There were five of them, the woman with the two kids that had fled the sandwich shop and a middle-aged couple. She could see the goo rising around their feet, their struggle to lift their legs against the strength of the substance. *Like flies on flypaper*, she thought, shuddering at the image. The woman with the two young kids had picked them up and teetered helplessly as she was held fast to the ground.

Moxy looked around helplessly, shouting for help but not knowing how anyone could. Then miraculously, help came. Grinding sickly and still venting steam, the pickup that had t-boned the police car came gliding onto the scene and stopped abruptly amidst the rising tide of deadly green sludge. The man in the mesh cap climbed awkwardly back out to his truck bed, and with surprising speed began pulling up the five trapped people.

Moxy could see shoes and socks left behind, disappearing beneath the slime as the last of the people were pulled up into the truck. But for all the haste the man had shown charging onto the scene, the slime was faster. A six-foot blister of it bubbled up a dozen or so feet from the front of the truck, and with the same slow impact it had against the building, it slammed into the front of the vehicle, crashing through the windshield and flooding the cab with its acidic juices.

The pool of the substance had radiated too wide for them to jump, but Moxy was inspired into action by the truck driver's heroism. She could see that quite a few nearby cars had stopped in the road, with drivers and onlookers congregating at the edge of the slime, testing it with hesitant footsteps and prodding.

Without a word, Moxy bolted to the nearest car, a Ford sedan of some variety. The driver, now a few feet from the open driver's side door was too slow to act as she dove in and threw the machine into drive. As soon as the tires hit the surface of the green gunk it felt like she had depressed the brakes, and she stomped the accelerator to continue forward even at a snail's pace.

The car slurped to a halt about four feet from the rear of the battered truck. Its occupants huddled at the rear of the truck bed, backing away as far as they could from the substance that now pulsed and oozed through the rear window.

From Moxy's vantage point she could see another conglomeration of the slime forming and tried anything to get her vehicle unmired from its sticky grip. It was no use, however, and as the heavy thuds of feet hit the hood of the car, she knew that at the very least she had bought everyone a little more time.

Strong hands hauled Moxy out of the car and up onto the roof of it. Huddled mostly on hands and knees, the group of them shouted and scrambled helplessly. The onlooking crowd took action and another vehicle was pulled out into the mire, forming another stepping stone across the dangerous surface of slime.

"That was good thinking," Moxy said to the man in the mesh hat when they had jumped down from the last vehicle and onto solid ground.

"Thanks for taking my lead. The name's Bob," he said breathlessly, elated to be moving away from the stuff.

Those of the survivors and of the crowd that were willing and able, rushed to the nearby buildings, shouting for people to evacuate. Before long Moxy spotted more law enforcement rushing onto the scene and behind them a van with the Argos Energy Group logo.

"Buck!" she shouted, waving him over as soon as there was a clearing for him to pull forward.

"Wow, this is chaos. Are you all right?" he asked

"Yeah, believe it or not, I am. I thought you were going to shoot the site full of biocide?"

"I am, it's spooled up," he said, gesturing to a laptop on the seat beside him, "The supercharged biocide injection is triggering as we speak."

Moxy looked out at the retreating waves of slime building up into one massive mound of the stuff, cresting nearly twenty feet in height.

"Maybe I was wrong, maybe the cats are out of the bag or it is just immune or something."

Then, without warning the giant bubble burst, sending globs of the substance in all directions, like a humungous volcano of Jell-O spewing acidic death.

This action proved to be the last as all cohesion seemed to release. They watched as the last of it pattered to the ground like rain, and all was still.

All manner of tests and searches were conducted after that day, and while the evidence and reports were ample, the slime that had wreaked so much damage and hurt so many people was not observed alive again.

With their testing complete and reports filed with the authorities Buck and Moxy were sent back to headquarters, and while they had recommended a robust set of tests and precautions be taken around the Michigan remote fracking post. None, were observed. Rebecca Herve was unwilling to entertain the thought of a connection between the events at Fife Lake and the Argos extraction site. "This company has already lost too much," was her only official statement.

On the positive side, Argos Energy Group has reported record profits this quarter and is poised to be the industry leader in small-scale remote oil extraction for the next decade.

Buck was able to attend his daughter's birthday party.

Moxy put in her two-week notice.

Another Line

by Melodie Bolt

At the Crystal Knob Quarry, Destiny Watchett rolled her Schwinn up to the rock everyone called 'the sofa' and dismounted her bike. The green banana seat of her Sting-Ray glittered with silver in the late afternoon sun. She dropped her kickstand and reached into her culottes' pocket and pulled out her strawberry Bonne Bell Lip Smacker. She carefully rolled it on then tucked it away.

Kempert Hillyer sat with his back to her, looking at the navy water in the quarry. His dirty blond feathers didn't have even a single hair out of place. His face reminded her a little of Shawn Cassidy. Shawn was cute, but she preferred Parker Stevenson. Still, there was something mysterious about this guy.

"Hi Kemp," she said and settled next to him. He tilted his head slightly but kept studying the water. Time passed slowly, and the silence unnerved her. Something was always happening at home. Her stepmom cleaning the casserole dish while watching *Mork and Mindy* or her brother listening to *Highway to Hell* repeatedly, making the wall between their bedrooms shake.

She interrupted the quiet. "So, what kind of music do you like? I'm a big fan of Donna Summer and Olivia Newton John."

He sighed. "The only thing I've found even slightly interesting right now is Funkadelic's *Uncle Jam Wants You*."

Destiny didn't know what to say to that. "How'd you end up in Richmond, Virginia of all places?"

He shrugged and motioned toward the quarry. "There was a forest here once."

Destiny frowned. "That musta been a long time ago."

"Only 800,000 years, or so ahead."

Destiny laughed. "You're funny." She touched brushed her fingertips against his forearm.

He frowned and looked, for a moment, like he'd smelled rotten chicken.

"Let's walk." His sneakers grated on the gravel as he stood then headed on a dirt path that led around the rim.

"Wait for me," she said and rushed to catch up with him. The summer sun beat down on the rocks: the dust, bitter on her lips.

At a small copse of trees, he slowed and waited for her.

"Gosh," she said, "I'm so hot. Maybe we should go skinny dipping?" She was terrified he'd say yes, but she really wanted to show up at the theater on Friday to see *Meatballs* with a boy on her arm. That would show Marie, Michelle, and Katie a thing or two.

"In another line, maybe."

"You mean, life?" Destiny said fanning herself. She looked around. There were a couple of logs near an ashy pit. An old upright Frigidaire squatted in piles of empty, scattered beer bottles. She noticed a log and sat down on it hoping there weren't any spiders and wiped a trickle of sweat from her forehead.

"I meant timeline." Kemp turned to look at her. His gaze was so intense, a quick chill gusted up her spine. "Why did you meet me here?"

"Because you asked me to." Heat kindled on her cheeks. "You're cute. And, I don't know, we could, you know, hang out and stuff."

"But you know so terribly little about me, and I of you, really."

Destiny laughed nervously. "You sound so old fashioned. Where'd you say you moved from?"

"Oh, I've always lived right around here since the Watchetts left England. But I've just moved back, you see. Just like pushing a clock's hand closer to the hour."

Destiny frowned a little. What did that mean? It didn't matter. Kemp was better than no boy at all. She was tired of the girls making fun of her being single. Sometimes their words cut her heart. So maybe, she thought, Kemp and I could make Jiffy Pop and watch the next episode of *The Six Million Dollar Man* tonight. She inhaled to ask, but he was still talking.

"…so, tell me, Destiny, how do I know you really do like me?"

"Cuz I rode my bike all the way here to meet you. It felt like 5 miles."

He raised an eyebrow briefly. "True. But how do I know that you'll love me forever?"

Destiny's heart fluttered along with her eyelashes. "Because I pinky swear," she held up her hand, little finger extended.

Kemp shook his head.

Destiny thought then shrugged. But an idea popped into her head unexpectedly like a mongoose on a seesaw. "Do you, you know..." The heat in her cheeks made her heart thunder. "...wanna kiss me?"

"No," he said. He held up his hands apologetically. "I was thinking more along the lines of trust, commitment, sacrifice. Not love making."

She giggled. "You talk so weird. Honestly, I'm fresh outta ideas."

"I know you are," he tried to cover a smile. "I want to test your loyalty, your commitment. Get in the ice box. I mean the Frigidaire."

"Okay, okay," she said moving toward it. But then that thing that her brain did, that buzz, sparked her mouth to blurt the most awful thing. "But why?" She quickly covered her mouth.

"You scared?" He opened the door.

She nodded but her mouth said "Nope." Then she took an inventory of what was inside. It was empty. She didn't want to go in there but the thought of her friends making fun on Friday, boyless again, burned her brain. She was a virgin still so she couldn't to get invited their sleepovers or sit at their lunch table. She wanted the name-calling to stop. She'd do whatever needed to be done. She'd show Kemp she wasn't afraid and that she believed in true love and roller skating just like in *Xanadu*. He closed the door. A rectangular hole had been cut in the front so she could see outside.

"Okay, so for how long?" she asked, her voice tinny.

"How about 800,000 years. How does that sound?"

"Well, will that be over by Friday? I'd really like you to take me to the movies." She felt nervous like she might puke or something. He'd let her out soon though. "I'd really like to see *Meatballs*, you know, 'cuz I hear its funny."

"I'm afraid this is goodbye, Destiny."

"We could go see *Moonraker* if you wanted to. I mean I don't even like that stupid movie's name I mean, why did they name it after spaghetti? It could have been, I don't know, like 'Bubble Gum' or something. You know, something cooler."

He didn't say anything, but she knew he was still there.

She decided she'd wait. She wouldn't show him she was scared even though she did have to pee a little.

The quarry was quiet except for the occasional crow spreading gossip. But as the sky bladed from Tang to magenta, she finally called out for him.

"Well," Kemp said, his obsidian eyes glittering. "You lasted a lot longer than the last Watchett woman I killed."

Killed? Destiny started crying then, rolling sounds like a small dog barking. Each time she blinked her eyes, everything just seemed worse and worse. She lied to her mom about being at Katie's house so she could meet up with a boy. A boy who didn't even taste her Lip Smacker flavor! She hadn't told anyone, anyone at all, where she was going. She was probably dead, she realized. Dead. Even if she lived through this, her dad would kill her. Would her brother even care? He'd probably just steal all her records, even the Beach Boys who he said he hated, but secretly liked. And that made her cries careen into keening. Long, low, and heartsick.

"But why, Kemp? Why?" She could hardly blubber out the words.

"Because a long time ago some woman in your family loved H. George Wells. And George didn't deserve to be loved. He left us there when he could have come back. We fought the Morlocks for him. And then he left. And then we lost. We lost everything. I am the very, very last Eloi. The only one. And, you see, if I feed the Morlocks, they won't come down this timeline now that they have their own time machine. That's our deal. I must send them someone. Why not you? You're so terribly dull; you have nothing to offer this world. Or any of them, really."

Gosh, she thought, this was more dramatic than anything she'd ever seen on T.V. — even *Dallas*. "But what about me? You have to let me out."

"Oh," he said as he backed away from the hole. "You'll be let out, but not by me."

And then the weirdest thing happened: it looked like Kemp just scooted up the hill like he was on a bike, but he wasn't. And then it was night, and then day, and then night. Then the cops came in a blur. With dogs. One of them looked right at her and bayed. But as the deputy drew close, he simply walked through her.

She screamed then. Her lungs shuddered as they heaved. She couldn't get enough air. She drew to the hole and watched as the trees shed and grew leaves, snow and rain fell, the water in the quarry dropped lower and lower. Someone cut down the trees, and made a large building, and then it became bigger, and then there were cars, but they didn't look right. There was no style, no character. And then beyond understanding the days and nights simply became smudged centuries that flickered into thousands of shards of grey. She stopped screaming and crying by then. Slowly, the world began to come back to itself. And when it was still, completely still, she blinked and looked into the darkness. Someone was breathing out there. Maybe more than one she realized. Maybe one of them could open the door. She pulled her lip gloss out and clenched it in her hand.

"Hello?' she whispered.

Dozens of eyes winked like silver flashlights.

The door opened with a thud. She closed her eyes and offered a prayer of thanks. The air felt refreshing, and she breathed in deeply. When she opened her eyes, she studied the white-haired people. The Morlocks Kemp had called them. Their faces looked like molded melted plastic. Their teeth –crooked and awful. Still, maybe they could take her to a phone and she could call her mom. But they grabbed a hold of her roughly and carried her into a pink ziggurat.

The room was full of bones. When she saw the skulls, she cried out and writhed. The Morlocks gripped her tighter and started pulling on her arms and legs. They pulled and pulled. She screamed. It hurt so bad. She wanted to go home again. She'd be a good girl and not wander away with boys. She'd try harder in school. She could feel her tendons ripping, her shoulder coming loose. She understood that there were no second chances. Blood spurted from where her arm had been. The Morlock holding her dismembered arm opened wide and pulled her bicep off with his horrid teeth. Her lip gloss rolled across the floor.

Substitute

by J.M. Van Horn

Rachel's absolute best feeling in the world was reading a book while curled up on the couch with her cat. A close second was how serene the middle school library felt when the day was over and the kids were gone.

She was busy at the primary computer, closing out the final daily tasks, when a shallow groan came from the back of the library. The clacking on the keyboard stopped. Rachel waited to see if it was a random noise. Another one confirmed it wasn't. She moved out from behind the desk in search of the owner.

When she reached the rarely used history section, she found the source of the groans. Davey, an eighth grader who would easily pass for an elementary school student because of his smaller stature. He was sitting on the floor, back pressed against the wall, and eyes closed.

Rachel stopped by the nearest bookshelf next to the student. "You okay Davey?"

"It hurts." Davey looked up, tears rolling down his cheeks, when his eyes opened.

She knelt down by the boy's side. "Where does it hurt, Davey?" A pungent odor emanated from him. It reminded Rachel of when a skunk had crept into her crawlspace and sprayed. A weird acidic mixture of rotten eggs and burnt garlic. She did her best to breathe through her mouth, but that was even threatening to make her gag.

He leaned forward and pulled his knees to his chest. Each breath grew deeper and the grey t-shirt tightened over his back.

"Everywhere."

Rachel hated it when any of the students were sick or in pain but at first glance, she couldn't see anything wrong with him. She reached out and placed her hand on his back. The shirt had turned damp with sweat and the skin was emitting a fiery heat.

"Don't touch me, bitch." Davey swatted at her hand and scrambled a few feet away. He crouched facing her. His dark gaze narrowed on her.

Davey shifted his weight and muscles tightened, priming his body to respond.

Rachel tried to steady her nerves as she stood up. A weakness in her knees crept through her body. She used the bookshelf to offer a little support. Last time someone called her a bitch was back in college when she ended up on the wrong side of town late one night. "Davey! There is no need to use language like that."

"Shut up before I make you." Davey grated his teeth together.

He was different now.

Gone was the thin, underdeveloped body barely at the edge of puberty.

It had been replaced with muscles and a sizable mass where they were previously lacking. The t-shirt bulged and rippled, giving way to nightmare fuel of deformed Nintendo characters. Any sign of innocence or a childhood in his face were long gone, replaced with a more threatening visage.

She was going to say something, to remain in control of the confrontation. Before she could utter another word, Davey reacted.

He lunged at her but underestimated his own speed. Arms flailed as he slammed into the bookcase next to her. It toppled down on top of Davey as books flew off the shelves and littered the floor.

Rachel yelped as she stumbled backward at the unexpected attack. She steadied herself and grabbed a few hardcover books in some sort of attempt at defense. They might have proved more useful when she threw them at the fallen attacker if she had more than an ounce of athletic ability.

Davey growled as he shoved the fallen bookcase off. The strewn books tossed aside as he grunted in Rachel's direction.

Rachel screamed as she raced toward the back office. The metal door was thick enough to keep anyone out. She could lock him out and call someone for help. Before she could reach for the door and safety, Davey slammed her body against the unforgiving metal surface. The impact was enough to erase any actual plan of action she had left. Rachel's last thought was the tight grip on her skull before it collided with the door again.

"Watch out!"

The harsh warning rang out down the halls, followed by a metal folding chair careening off the wall. Henry dropped to the floor with the grace of a fish flopping out of water. Twisting around on the linoleum, he saw the gym teacher scrambling down the hall toward him. He couldn't remember the man's name, but the chair hurler lumbering toward him easily distracted him.

Their purser was a perplexing sight. It was maybe five feet tall, but built like a brick house and covered in typical garb for a middle school student. It might have been enough to elicit a laugh on any other day, but the dictionary flying past his head quelled that thought.

Henry hightailed it back to the place that had been home for the last few days, the science classroom. The pairs of heavy footsteps behind meant the others were following.

When the gym teacher crossed the threshold behind him, Henry slammed the classroom door shut and leaned his weight against it. The other man moved into position and dropped to his knees, where he fumbled around with the floor barricade until it slipped into place. Three seconds later, their purser made his presence known and slammed into the door. The barricade did its job and didn't give an inch.

Henry braced his back against the door. Despite the supposed touting power of the barricade, he felt extra support couldn't hurt. "What the hell is that?"

"You mean who? And it was Davey Wright." The gym teacher looked up at him and parted his lips, but nothing came right away. "Shit, you are the sub for Mrs. Brown's science class?"

Henry nodded as a rhythmic pounding continued against the classroom door. They showed no signs of slowing down.

The gym teacher winced as he examined his left hand. There was some slight redness along the edge, not to mention his ring and pinky fingers were angled in the wrong direction.

"Did he?" Henry asked, gesturing to the man's busted hand.

Davey continued to emit low growls between the pounding on the door. Every so often, the men would hear something being grunted under his breath.

"Yes, but it looks worse than it is." The gym teacher stood up and leaned against a nearby desk. "Wish I could say the same for Rachel."

"Who?" Henry's lost in the forest look accompanied the question.

"Right, a sub." The gym teacher walked around the room, opening drawers and cupboards, hoping to find anything useful. He found a roll of painters tape that fit the bill. He bound the broken fingers together in a methodical motion, forcing himself to hurry even when the pain grew. A few tears had been blinked away by the time he finished, over half of the tape roll was gone. This left the man with what looked like the reverse of the foam finger.

"She was a library assistant. I was heading home when I heard some screams from the library." A deep sigh slipped past his lips. "By the time I got there, it was too late. Some blood on the office door and she was on the ground, not moving. Davey was standing over her with the same chair he threw at you."

The pounding on the door had stopped, followed by a rough chuckle.

"She didn't listen."

Both men glanced toward the door when the relentless pounding started back up. The gym teacher nodded to the back of the room where the teacher's desk was situated. The room's second door was to the left of the massive whiteboard, which had "Nature vs. Nurture" scrawled across it. Both men huddled closer together to ensure there were no more prying ears.

The gym teacher leaned in. "You know where the Hyde patches are?"

"No frigging clue. Thought that was a bad training video."

A perplexed look overtook the man's pained features. "You haven't lived in Michigan long, have you?"

Henry shook his head. "Sorry, I just moved here this past summer."

"Well, shit." The gym teacher paced in small circles around the desk. He was gingerly holding his left hand. The swelling around the joints and the angry red color of his skin contrasted with the painters tape band-aid. More and more, it looked like something out of a cartoon. "The patches came out about three years ago after the third incident with a Hyde kid happened outside of Lansing."

Henry jerked his thumb to the classroom door that was still under assault by Davey. "There were more like this?"

The gym teacher gave a curt nod. "Not sure how many, lost count." He held his injured hand above his heart, hoping to reduce some of the swelling. "It turns out, about fifteen years ago, a whack of a doctor made sure the sperm banks across the state were stocked up on his swimmers. What made it worse was there was something 'special' about them. He supposedly altered his genes to remove any genetic behavior disorders."

Henry chortled. "That's not even possible yet. That kind of stuff you only see in science fiction movies."

The gym teacher managed a shrug of sorts. "I would say the same thing, but tell him that." The cartoon hand pointed toward the door.

"Either way, he screwed something up, and it has the opposite effect. It brings out the worst behaviors."

Henry moved closer to the man. "How did they figure this out?"

"No clue. They supposedly found a few of the kids by luck before anything happened. But some potential parents had no desire to offer any blood sample for testing. They did not want the government or anyone else taking their kids."

"Can't blame them." Henry started to pace back and forth in a six-step pattern.

The gym teacher stopped mid-stride and barked out a laugh. "Not much for public safety, huh?"

"Open up!" The banging on the door intensified. Each hit from Davey was stronger and harder. Both men watched how the floor barricade handled each blow with not so much of a twitch.

The men moved into a tighter conspirator circle. "What are we supposed to do now? Sneak out? Or wait for some kind of help?"

"Eventually Davey will try to figure out another way in and that will be a lot sooner than any kind of help to arrive." The gym teacher winced when his injured hand nipped the edge of the desk. "Look, between the two of us, we can handle him."

"You mean one and a half?"

"Not funny, and he got the jump on me before. If we can get a Hyde patch on an exposed part of his skin, he'll be out in no time."

"Sorry, coping mechanism." Henry titled his head toward the man. "Are you sure it works?"

"We don't have any other choices. Don't think we're going to have enough time until he calms down."

The men were reminded of their problem with a series of punches reverberating against the metal door.

"Damn, he is relentless." Henry looked back toward the door. "Guess not. Any suggestions on the best way to do this?"

"Keep him busy and I'll be back in a minute at most." The gym teacher moved along the back wall. He gave a quick thumbs up to Henry and slipped out of the room.

Henry glanced back at the door. The pounding had waned. There was less force behind each one. That definitely was not a good sign. He hurried over to the door and stopped a few feet from the opening.

What was his name? They had already said it a couple of times. More of a reminder that his memory was crap. It didn't help with all the students he had met over the last couple of days.

"Calm down," Henry muttered through dry lips.

A loud slam was the response to the weak request. A motivational plague, "Today's Learners, Tomorrow's Leaders," fell off the wall. "Don't tell me to call down." Davey growled.

Henry nodded, more out of a reminder for himself. Billy? Jimmy? Stevie? Finally, the name came to him. "Davey, we can figure it out.

"What makes you so smart?" Davey snorted.

"You have no idea." Henry rolled his eyes, a comment he heard countless times from his parents while he was growing up. "If I open the door, can we talk?"

The pounding instantaneously stopped, and the room fell silent.

"Talk?" Davey's voice softened to the point. He sounded like a kid struggling with a sore throat.

Henry looked over his shoulder at the back door. No sign of the gym teacher yet. Maybe his way would work and he would get him to calm down. Besides, the man said he should be back in a minute. "Give me a couple of seconds to move the barricade and get away from the door." No response came to his request. "Remember, I can't help if you knock me into the wall or worse."

The planned execution went as smoothly as could be. The barricade was removed, and he found a spot behind a few desks and chairs with little of a sound. Before the door opened, the handle on the door jiggled, and Davey stepped into the room.

Henry had a better chance to look at Davey and found himself even more in awe than he was at first glance. He would have never guessed the beast in front of him was a 13-year-old boy. He would have guessed Davey was in his mid-thirties with a history of weightlifting and plenty of bar fights. The smell of rotten garlic drifted in with him, forcing Henry's eyes to water.

Davey clenched his eyes and grasped at his left shoulder and another hand on his chest. Sweat dripped from his face. He staggered forward a step, but righted himself.

Henry took a step closer, keeping a couple of desks between them. "What's wrong?"

"It hurts all over. My skin feels like it is burning, ripping apart." He grunted and clenched his jaw, attempting to shut down the pain. Davey made a fist and brought it down on the center of a student desk. The impact cracked the particleboard top and forced the metal legs to bend outwards.

"I know…" Henry moved around the makeshift barricade. He knew showing trust in Davey was going to be the best way to make a strong connection.

"Stop it…" Davey snapped. "She didn't listen and look at what happened." A thick chuckle punctuated the point. "And you don't know." He grabbed the fire extinguisher off the nearby wall and hurled it at Henry. The metal cylinder missed the target and crashed into the nearby desks.

Henry did not stop his forward progress, but shortened the distance between his steps. "Oh, I do. Shame I was never a sub for your science class, then you might understand."

"Talk, talk, talk." Davey glared at him. "You talk too much." A smile crept across his contorted face. He lunged across the desks, arms outstretched for Henry.

Henry underestimated how fast Davey was and especially how far he could jump. The two collided when Henry cleared the last desk. Even though Henry had a good twelve inches and about seventy pounds advantage on Davey, he was struggling. The two wrestled to gain the upper hand and keep things under control. Back and forth they went, tumbling over chairs and banging into desks.

Henry was not even sure when the gym teacher returned to the room. All he saw was the thick forearm slip from behind Davey and try to lock itself in place around the boy's neck. Henry felt the tide was turning, but he was not sure if it was going to be in the right direction. Then he saw the man's plan fail.

Davey worked enough space between the forearm and his neck. He opened his maw wide and clamped down with all his might. The gym teacher screamed as he yanked his arm back. He was haphazardly tossed into the mass of classroom furniture. Davey spit out a chunk of flesh, blood, and various fibrous connective tissues.

"It's on. Hold him!" The gym teacher called out from somewhere in the room. Each word filled with more pain and anguish.

The adrenaline teetering on the edge offered Henry one last surge. It was enough to lock his fingers behind Davey's back and encase him in a bear hug. He squeezed harder, even as the mass of muscles continued to work against him. During the struggle, their eyes locked, and that is when Henry thought the Hyde patch failed.

Instead, Davey's eyes dimmed, and his eyelids grew heavy. The medications took over and soon Davey was dead weight in Henry's grasp. He lowered him to the floor among the destructive scene.

"Rest easy Davey." A vocal groan reminded Henry that the gym teacher needed some help.

Henry caught sight of the nearby fire extinguisher among the scattered debris. He grabbed the top of it and used it as support as he stood back up. It had been a long time before he used some of those muscles, but he felt good.

The gym teacher rolled onto his back and stole a glance to the sprawled out Davey. "Good job."

"Appreciate the help. There was no way I could've done it without you." Henry reached back and brought the end of the half-filled canister down into the gym teacher's forehead. The man's forehead split and blood splattered with the impact. A second swing was enough to crack the man's skull. The man went limp, his cartoon hand twitching.

Henry decided another half dozen hits or more were enough to make sure the gym teacher's days were done and over. The blood covered extinguisher dropped to the carpet with a dull thud. Henry turned back to the slumbering Davey.

Henry walked back to the young man and wiped his hands against his slacks. He measured each movement and, with one fluid motion, bent at his knees to scoop up Davey. Henry could feel the boy's heart beat slowly against his chest. "Time to go find your brothers and sisters."

Henry never had been one for paternal instincts, but things could change in time.

Contributing Authors

Peggy Christie ("The Dreadful Sisters Who Remain") is an author of horror and dark fiction. Her work has appeared in dozens of websites, magazines, and anthologies. Her horror fiction/art collaboration with Don England, *Plague of Man: SS of the Dead*, can be found through Amazon; her short story collections, *Dark Doorways* and *Hell Hath No Fury*, from Dragons Roost Press; and her vampire novel, *The Vessel*, from Source Point Press. Peggy is one of the founding members of the Great Lakes Association of Horror Writers, as well as a contributing writer for the website of Cinema Head Cheese. Check out her webpage at themonkeyisin.com for more information on her other publications and appearances.

Peggy loves Korean dramas, survival horror video games, and chocolate (not necessarily in that order) and lives in Michigan with her husband.

M.C. St. John ("These Things Move in Cycles") is a writer living in Chicago. He is the author of the short story collection *Other Music*. His stories have appeared, as if by luck or magic, in *Burial Day Books*, *Dark Ink Books*, *Nightscript*, *Flame Tree Publishing*, and *Wyldblood Press*. He is also a member of the Great Lakes Association of Horror Writers, serving as co-editor for the horror anthology *Recurring Nightmares*. See what he's writing next at www.mcstjohn.com.

R D Doan ("An Eye for Beauty"), a member of the Great Lakes Association of Horror Writers, has had short stories appear online on sites such as burialday.com and in *The Sirens Call* eZine. His tales of horror have also been featured in the anthologies *Dark Carnival*, *Marisa's Recurring Nightmares*, *Nobody Goes Out Anymore: Futuristic Fiction Post Covid-19*, *Angela's Recurring Nightmares*, *Thuggish Itch: By the Seaside*, and *Bag of Bones 206 Word Stories*. As a

Physician Assistant, he has authored the Textbook *Evidence-based Medicine on the Trail* and has written numerous academic articles, but he prefers to wade into the world of darker fiction. He resides in West Michigan with his wife, two sons and dogs.

He can be found online on Twitter (@rd3_pac) and Instagram (@rddoan).

Jen Haeger ("That Won't Hold Up In Court") hails from southeast Michigan and is a veterinarian turned forensic science masters student turned master beekeeper and author. Her publications include a future detective thriller series, paranormal romance trilogy, post-apocalyptic sick-kid novel, paranormal thriller novelette, and two short horror stories. Additionally, four of her short stories have been awarded an honorable mention in the Writers of the Future Contest. When not writing, Jen can be found in her apiary tending to colonies of stinging insects with her mother-in-law, out hiking in the wilderness with her ever-supportive husband, or acting as a couch for her two cats while reading a good book. Intrigued? Find out more at www.jenhaeger.com or stalk me on Facebook (Jen Haeger) or Twitter (@JenHaeger).

Matthew Tansek ("No Country for Old Blobs") is a Detroit area writer and librarian who loves to bring the excitement of speculative fiction to new audiences. After a decade of working with books, Matt knows what makes a good story- and it's not five-dollar words or trendy subject matter. It's compelling characters in evocative situations. Information about Matthew and his works can be found at http://www.matthewtansek.com.

Melodie Bolt ("Another Line") recently published a poem in Black Spot Books' women of horror anthology *Under Her Skin*. Next year, Black Spot will also feature another poem in *Under Her Eye*. In October 2022, *Death's Garden Revisited* will include a personal essay about Melodie visiting Lenin's mausoleum. Melodie lives in Flint, Michigan with her partner, a black cat named Nyx, and a pack of dogs.

J.M. Van Horn ("Substitute") thwarts criminals during the day and writes a blend of horror and urban fantasy at night. The best kind of horror is the one you never see coming. Any free time is spent with his incredible wife and amazing son who are his driving force. Well that and some of the absolutely absurd dreams/nightmares he has. There are endless levels of horror.

His published works can be found in various places like *Sirens Call, Erie Tales, Ghostlight Magazine,* and more. You can find him through https://linktr.ee/JMVanHorn

Michael Cieslak (Editor) is a lifetime reader and writer of horror, mystery, and speculative fiction. A native of Detroit, he still lives within 500 yards of the city with his wife and their two dogs Tesla and Titus. The house is covered in Halloween decorations in October and dragons the rest of the year. He is an officer in the Great Lakes Association of Horror Writers and is the editor of the Erie Tales anthologies. His works have appeared in a number of collections including *DOA: Extreme Horror, Dead Science, Vicious Verses and Reanimated Rhymes*, the GLAHW anthologies, *Alter Egos Vol 1, Pan's Guide for New Pioneers* (a supplement for the Pugmire RPG), and the collaborative steampunk novel *Army of Brass. Urbane Decay*, a collection of Michael's short fiction, was released in 2018 by Source Point Press. He reviews horror movies for the Dean On Movie Reviews podcast.

Michael is the Editor in Chief of Dragon's Roost Press (thedragonsroost.biz).

Michael's mental excreta (including his personal blog They Napalmed My Shrubbery This Morning) can be found on-line at thedragonsroost.net.

Don England (Cover Artist) is a Michigan based artist specializing in creepy and macabre art for the last 25 years. He is a product of late-night eighties television, comic book shops, and classic rock music. Donald is a life-long collector of comic books and movie posters from which he draws his inspiration. In the nineties, he co-created the comic *Lethal Lita* with Michael Leblanc, and worked on other comics like *Tales from the Ravaged Lands*. By the end of the nineties, he was primarily working on horror projects, creating catalog cover art for VHS sellers like Video Wasteland and Video Dungeon. Over the years, his work has been seen in a number of magazines like *Horror Hound* and *Liquid Cheese*, as well as cover art for Evilspeak. His art has been featured in *Late Night Snack*, *The Thing* and *Stranger Things* art books, *Deadworld*, *Cromwell Green*, and on the covers of *Erie Tales*, *A Fist full of Dead Folk*, and *Night Pieces*. He's also completed t-shirt designs for Pallbearer Press and Rotten Cotton. For more info, visit http://www.donaldengland.com/ or find him on Facebook and Instagram.

About GLAHW

Great Lakes Association of Horror Writers (GLAHW) is a collective and compendium of writers, fans, and misshapen children all huddled together to share their love of Horror, Dark Fantasy, Sci-fi, True Crime, and the occasional Horotica. We love words to death.

Erie Tales is an annual publication dedicated stretching the imaginations of members. The theme is different every year.

Erie Tales is debuted at the Annual Monster Mash for Literacy Bash, and the proceeds from the party are generously donated to the Dominican and Siena Literacy Organizations of Detroit.

For more information on our group, activities and where to donate bail money, please visit us:

Facebook: https://www.facebook.com/GLAHW
Twitter: https://twitter.com/GLAHW
Website: http://www.glahw.com

Made in the USA
Monee, IL
01 February 2025